He swallowed.

Damn.

Her hair was different, which was why he hadn't recognized her from behind, but it was definitely her. A ghost from his past.

His distant past. He had to remind himself of that fact as his feet began moving again. What the hell was she doing here?

She'd sworn she was shaking the dust of Forgotten Point off her feet and never coming back. The last he'd heard from her mom was that she was a military doctor stationed somewhere in the Middle East.

Mysti looked just as shocked as he was as Tom made the introductions.

She nodded. "Yes. We've met."

He stared at her. Her voice was the same. The slight rough huskiness hit him in the gut, just like it had that night. But, like her hair, the tone was different. Tighter. Chillier.

"Yes," he agreed. "We have. We were in high school together, but it's been, what? Fifteen years?"

Dear Reader,

Have you ever felt the need to get away from a situation? To run as far and as fast as you can without looking back? Well, Mysti North finds herself in just such a situation. And she does exactly that: she runs. But sometimes the past has a funny way of catching up with you when you least expect it.

Thank you for joining Mysti and Jesse Grove as they unravel the decisions they made when they were younger versions of themselves and try to figure out where to go from there. And maybe, just maybe they can find what they lost all those years ago.

I hope you enjoy reading about their journey as much as I loved writing it.

Love,

Tina Beckett

STARTING OVER WITH THE SINGLE DAD

———

TINA BECKETT

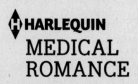

HARLEQUIN

MEDICAL
ROMANCE

HARLEQUIN®
MEDICAL
ROMANCE™

Recycling programs
for this product may
not exist in your area.

ISBN-13: 978-1-335-40881-5

Starting Over with the Single Dad

Copyright © 2021 by Tina Beckett

This edition published by arrangement with Harlequin Books S.A.

For questions and comments about the quality of this book,
please contact us at CustomerService@Harlequin.com.

Harlequin Enterprises ULC
22 Adelaide St. West, 40th Floor
Toronto, Ontario M5H 4E3, Canada
www.Harlequin.com

Printed in U.S.A.

Three-times Golden Heart® Award finalist **Tina Beckett** learned to pack her suitcases almost before she learned to read. Born to a military family, she has lived in the United States, Puerto Rico, Portugal and Brazil. In addition to traveling, Tina loves to cuddle with her pug, Alex, spend time with her family and hit the trails on her horse. Learn more about Tina from her website or friend her on Facebook.

Books by Tina Beckett

Harlequin Medical Romance

The Island Clinic collection

How to Win the Surgeon's Heart

New York Bachelor's Club

Consequences of Their New York Night
The Trouble with the Tempting Doc

A Summer in São Paulo

One Hot Night with Dr. Cardoza

A Family to Heal His Heart
A Christmas Kiss with Her Ex-Army Doc
Miracle Baby for the Midwife
Risking It All for the Children's Doc
It Started with a Winter Kiss

Visit the Author Profile page
at Harlequin.com for more titles.

To my husband.
I'm so glad that chance brought us together.

PROLOGUE

THE KISS CAME out of nowhere. And Lord, it was so incredibly heady. Decadent, even. Her lips clung to his warm mouth in desperation, her heart pounding in her chest. And Mysti North couldn't get enough.

She'd never dreamed her goodbye news would get this kind of a reaction from her childhood friend. But things had changed between them recently, and she couldn't stay in town with the way things were now.

The rain pounded down on the car and thunder cracked around them, but it couldn't reach inside and stop what was happening.

Mysti's arms slid around his neck, and a tiny sound emerged from her throat before she could stop it. Jesse's reaction was immediate. He pulled her even closer, tongue edging forward to meet hers and tangle with it.

Her world changed colors for several heart-stopping seconds.

The boy next door had morphed into a hunky high school quarterback four years ago, and suddenly girls had flocked around him. Including her best friend, Kandid. And Kandid was everything Mysti wasn't. Beautiful, poised, a cheerleader and confident in her own feminine powers of attraction, she'd set her sights on Jesse almost immediately after Mysti had confided in her friend about her own crush on him, and of course she'd emerged the victor. He and Kandid had been dating for several months now, her friend regaling Mysti with stories of their intimate talks about the future. Which included children.

Mysti had never even dreamed she might have a chance with him herself. Until this very moment.

Jesse had had to stop the car when the rain turned torrential, the weather reports of flash floods holding true as water rushed across the small bridge that led into their hometown. He'd said he didn't dare cross that line and risk the consequences.

But he had dared to cross another kind of line—by kissing her. And it had brought the smoldering spark of hope inside her blazing back to life.

He'd offered to give her a ride home from the last game of their high school careers to save her mom from making the trip in the rain. And as she'd thrown her clarinet into the back seat, she'd decided that this was her chance to say a private goodbye to him. In person. Without the crowd that normally revolved around him. She'd already talked to a local army recruiter about her options and they, at least, seemed eager to have her.

So when he'd pulled over, she'd turned to him, clutching her hands in her lap and willing herself to make this final break. To give herself permission to walk away from her role of standing on the sidelines with the rest of Jesse's adoring public and find out what life held for her outside this town. Life without Jesse.

What she hadn't expected was the look that had crossed his face when she'd told him about her decision to join the army. "You're leaving Forgotten Point?"

"I am. I don't think this town holds much in the way of a future for me."

Especially not when all she could foresee was Jesse marrying Kandid and then forever having to meet him with a band on his finger that marked him as someone else's. Her friend's husband. But, God, how could she move away and leave him behind? He'd been a constant in her childhood, and to imagine him with anyone else hurt her beyond all imagining…

Except she'd never even dreamed of him staring at her like he had after she'd told him of her decision. But when he'd suddenly reached for her, she'd responded immediately, all of her repressed feelings flaring to life in an instant. She could call that recruiter and tell him she was no longer interested, couldn't she?

His fingers toyed with top button on her white shirt, and she sensed more than felt his hesitation. As if he were contemplating what going any further than this might mean.

Do it, Jesse. Please! Choose me.

Just then something seared the backs of her eyelids and she jerked them open, finding that another car had pulled up beside them, blue lights flashing. Jesse reeled back in his seat, shock and horror clearly written across his face.

Had he forgotten who he was kissing? Had he pictured Kandid sitting here with him, instead of her?

She recognized one of the town's patrol

cars. The door opened and out stepped Andy McGee, a flashlight in his hand. He came around to Jesse's window and used the torch to tap on it, rain streaming over the plastic that covered his hat and plopping onto his rainproof slicker. Jesse's eyes closed for a second before he seemed to straighten in his seat.

As he rolled down his window, bile crawled up Mysti's throat, and she waited for the lecture she was sure was coming. All she wanted to do right now was get out of this car and run into her bedroom. So much for hoping that Jesse had finally understood he was supposed to be with her, rather than Kandid.

"You kids aren't thinking of drivin' 'cross that bridge, now, are you?"

"No sir. I was just waiting for the rain to slow."

Andy leaned down farther to peer in at Mysti, and she wrapped her arms around her middle, suddenly freezing cold, although it had to be close to eighty degrees outside. Her eyes met Andy's for a second before skipping away again.

"Your folks know where you are, Mysti?"

"Yes, sir. Jess was just giving me a ride home. Then the rain struck and…"

"Got it." He tapped the side of the car. "It's dangerous sitting here like this, and the rain is only just starting to let up. I'll lead you back to Forgotten Point another way and get you home safe."

Home. She suddenly realized this was not her home. Not anymore.

"Okay, thanks."

Jesse waited until Andy got back into his vehicle, and then turned and pulled out behind the patrol car.

He glanced at her quickly, the appalled look in his eyes making her cringe inside. "Damn it, Myst. I am so sorry. Your friendship means more to me than anything. My dad…hell, I hope you know I would never even think of—"

"Don't say it." She forced herself to stop him as an almost overwhelming pain burst through her. Jesse's dad had cheated on his mom over and over, then abandoned his family, leaving his son to do his best to hold things together. The fact that he could even think he was anything like that horrible man…

She forced herself to continue, the shakiness of her words making her close her eyes briefly to try to pull herself together. "You are *nothing* like your father, Jess. Let's just pretend none of this ever happened, okay?"

Easier said than done. She had a feeling she was going to relive this kiss for many years to come. It had been good. So very good. The kind of kiss she'd dreamed of happening between her and Jesse. Had often prayed for. But not like this. Not with the feelings of guilt it would carry with it. As much as she'd hated that Kandid was dating Jesse, her friend couldn't help who she fell in love with. Everyone loved Jesse.

Everyone…including Mysti.

But no more. She wasn't going to sit around this small town and let her sadness fester until she became a bitter shell of a person. If she could do some good in this world she was going to take the opportunity. And right now, the army seemed like the perfect place to do that.

Her stomach clenched hard as she braced herself for what she knew was coming as they wound their way through country roads that led into Forgotten Point. Jesse didn't say anything else until he pulled up in front of Mysti's house.

She didn't want him to try to apologize again, so she yanked on the door handle, and the mechanism made a snapping sound that jarred her to the core. Then, before she opened the door, she heaved down a breath and prayed for the courage to make this final break. Turning to look at him, his haunted gaze made her throat ache with unshed tears.

"Bye, Jess."

She forced a finality into those two words that she didn't want to contemplate. Didn't want to accept.

But right here, right now, she was drawing her own line in the sand. Jesse belonged to someone else. He was on one side of that line, and she was on the other.

He wasn't, and nor would he ever be...hers.

CHAPTER ONE

Present day

MYSTI TOOK ONE last look at the gray building as she tossed her duffel bag into the taxi and climbed in after it. After six months of getting counseling for what was deemed PTSD, she'd finally graduated back to real life. She guessed she should have bought an actual suitcase as her time in the military came to an end, but who knew where life would take her next. For right now, though, she was going home. A place she'd always sworn she'd never go back to.

But a long time had passed since she'd made that vow. And what she'd endured in Joronha made the silliness of her first crush and her first-ever kiss seem like something out of a romantic comedy. Except none of it had been funny, and she hadn't gotten her happy ending. Just the ending.

So why go back to Forgotten Point?

Because she needed to. At least for this next phase of her life. She required the stable routine that Forgotten Point had always managed to give her. She smiled. She'd once been so contemptuous of that stability. The lack of surprises. She'd wanted so badly to do things that were reckless…see the bigger world outside her small town. Well, the first of those two wishes had happened in the front seat of Jesse Grove's car. And the second had happened on a series of foreign battlefields. Neither of those experiences had turned out quite the way she'd envisioned they might. So right now, Forgotten Point, Kentucky, looked very attractive. And safe. Far from the trauma of exploding helicopters and lost friends. The offer to take over for a surgeon who was on maternity leave at a hospital on the other side of the bridge from Forgotten Point had come at the perfect time for Mysti. And the fact that it wasn't a "forever" job made it that much more attractive to her. She didn't know yet how she would feel about the town once she got home.

The taxi driver glanced in the rearview mirror. "Where to?"

She managed a smile that was a lot less shaky than it had been when she'd first landed back on American soil. "To the air-port, please."

"You've got it."

As the cab pulled away from the building, she turned around and took one last look at it. So many years of her life had been spent following orders, she wasn't quite sure what to do now that she could choose for herself exactly where she went and how long she stayed.

Jesse would probably still be living in her hometown, although her mom had never once mentioned him during their texts. It was as if she'd known that her daughter had cared deeply about him and had somehow been hurt because of it, and hadn't wanted to add to that sorrow.

She shook her head and leaned back against the seat, closing her eyes. That part of her life was over. The last she'd heard—by means of Kandid's fancy hand-addressed wedding in-vitation—was that she and Jesse had indeed gotten married. But Mysti had never RSVP'd, and she and Kandid had soon lost touch. The same way she'd purposely lost touch with all her other childhood friends. They were all re-minders of what could have been.

Kandid and Jesse were probably still hap-pily living their lives together.

Well, it was time that Mysti finally started living hers. Her mom was so excited that she was coming home. Mysti had asked her to keep it quiet for now. She needed a few days to get her bearings and hopefully find a temporary place to live before people started dropping off pies and coming over to welcome her back. She could stay with her mom, but really, she needed her own space to continue to heal from the trauma of losing her friend in the field a year ago.

And she needed to brace herself for the time when she would eventually run into Jesse and his wife. She wished she'd gotten more closure on that whole childhood crush thing. Because right now there was a rock in the pit of her belly that was the size of a boulder.

Hell, he might not even recognize her. She'd lost weight over the ensuing years due to the busy hours spent operating on injured soldiers and the trauma she'd endured at the end of her last tour. Her mom would fuss over her, and she'd gain everything back, and probably more in short order.

Well, there was time enough to think of all of that once she got on the ground and started work. Until then, she needed to do what her counselor had told her. Take one day at a time. Focus on moving forward a little bit each day.

Until the past year was a distant blur she could no longer see so clearly in her mind's eye.

Jesse helped his patient sit upright on the table, noting her wince as she did so. She hadn't mentioned her previous L2 compression fracture as her reason for visiting today, but he could see it was still bothering her. "How's your back doing, Mrs. Evans?"

Gertrude Evans had been one of his teachers in high school. Now well into her seventies, she was retired and living alone at home, her husband having passed away last year.

"The pain is still there, but as long as I don't try to stay bent over for too long, we get by." Despite the arthritis pain that sometimes plagued her, she was surprisingly healthy. Healthy enough to still get out and tend to her animals and small farm with some help from her sons. The compression fracture had been the result of a fall from a ladder while adjusting a gutter on her house, which she'd insisted could happen to anyone. And she was right.

Although Jesse's real love was caring for

elderly patients like Mrs. Evans, he was glad that med school had required him to specialize in internal medicine before he went on to his fellowship in geriatric medicine.

When his grandmother had been struck down by a mystery illness, there'd been no one at the hospital who'd specialized in geriatrics. Oh, her medical care had been above reproach, but it had been hard to get to the root of the problem, since her early dementia had made it hard for her to sort her symptoms in the order they'd appeared.

Jesse had already been in medical school by that time, and had planned to specialize in orthopedics. His grandmother's illness had made him switch tracks. And he'd had no regrets about that decision. But the truth was that the hospital wouldn't have hired him on as a geriatrics specialist alone. This wasn't Florida or one of the other retirement meccas.

"Well, you let me know if it starts getting worse and we'll come up with some other treatment options for you."

"Thank you, Jesse, but I suspect I'll just work through it myself in time. Everything else looks good?"

"Yes. Your lab results came back just fine."

Gertie slid from the table with an ease that

would put some forty-year-olds to shame. "How's your girl doing? I haven't heard about her in a while."

He stiffened for a second before he realized she was talking about his daughter. "She's just fine. Starting third grade this fall."

"They grow up so fast." She crammed her feet into footwear that made him smile. People swore those hole-riddled plastic shoes were incredibly comfortable, but somehow they seemed incongruous on someone like Gertie. Then again, she never had been one to follow the crowd, even as a teacher, which had made her very popular with her students.

"That they do." He glanced at the planner on his phone. "I want to check on your back again to make sure it's not getting worse. We'll set your next appointment for six months out, but call if you notice something before then."

"I will, thanks."

He walked her out to the reception area and said goodbye before ducking out into the hallway. The medical office building was housed in an annex of the Serenity Regional Medical Center itself. It made it convenient when it came to doing rounds of patients he had at the hospital, especially during inclement weather, or on days like today when he was going to pop into the cafeteria for a quick bite to eat.

The double doors that connected his wing with the hospital opened with a whisper of sound, and he went through them, his mind running through all the things he needed to do before he picked up Sally from school this afternoon.

He spied Tom, the hospital administrator, across the lobby talking to someone. Jesse gave him a short wave, but Tom gestured for him to come over. He did, his smile instinctively including the other person who'd turned around to see who Tom was motioning to. Jesse stopped in his tracks.

Surely that wasn't…

He swallowed.

Damn.

Her hair was different, which was why he hadn't recognized her from behind, but it was definitely her. Mysti North. A ghost from his past.

His distant past. He had to remind himself of that fact as his feet began moving again. What the hell was she doing here?

She'd sworn she was shaking the dust of Forgotten Point off her feet and never com-

ing back. The last he'd heard from her mom
several years ago was that Mysti had qualified as a military doctor and was being stationed somewhere in the Middle East.

Mysti looked just as shocked as he was as
Tom made the introductions.

She nodded. "Yes. We've met."

Jesse stared at her. Her voice was just the
same. The slight rough huskiness hitting
him in the gut, just like it had that night. But
like her hair, the tone was different. Tighter.
Chillier.

"Yes," he agreed. "We have. We were in
high school together, but it's been, what?
Fifteen years since you left?"

"Something like that." Her stiff smile
as she glanced between him and Tom contained no warmth. Just a cool indifference
that seemed so out of character with the person he'd once known.

"Great!" Tom said enthusiastically. "Are
you in a hurry, Jesse?"

"No, I was actually just going to grab a
bite to eat."

"Would you mind showing Dr. North
around the hospital? The cafeteria would
be a good place to start."

Dr. North. Oh, hell, Tom had used her
title. Was she going to be working here? He

should have known when his day started off as well as it had that there was bound to be a downside somewhere along the way.

What could he say? No, he didn't want to show her around? Didn't want her working here?

Both of those things were true. But if he said so, the next time he saw Tom, there would be some uncomfortable questions asked. Questions he'd rather not answer.

"Of course." He sent an inquiring glance to Mysti. "Have you eaten yet?"

"No, but I don't want to hold you up. Seriously."

She sounded just as reluctant to spend time with him as he felt.

"Nonsense," Tom said briskly. "I'm sure Jesse wouldn't have asked if he didn't want you to join him."

That just went to show that his hospital administrator didn't known him as well as he thought he did.

"Of course not." He forced another smile, feeling it shrink to match the reluctant vibes Mysti was giving off in waves. She obviously didn't want anything to do with him. Hell, he couldn't blame her.

He'd been dating Mysti's friend for a couple of months when that kiss in his car had happened. And although he and Kandid hadn't been serious about each other at the time, he'd still felt like he'd cheated on her. It just went to show that Jesse was indeed capable of acting exactly like his father, something he never would have dreamed possible before that night. So he'd failed as a boyfriend—and he hadn't done such a great job of being a husband, either.

"Well, I'll leave you two to it, then, since I have a meeting in about twenty minutes. Thanks, Jesse."

"Not a problem, Tom."

But it was, although he wasn't sure why. What had happened between them was a long time ago. They'd both moved on with their lives. He'd married Kandid, and Mysti had joined the military. They were past those juvenile hormones that came with being a teenager.

Was this why you went into geriatrics? To remove the temptation of ever getting married again? You don't exactly meet many women your age...

The words slithered through his head, winding around his brain cells in a way that made him frown. No, he'd gone into that branch of medicine because of his grandmother. He'd never cheated on Kandid in all their years of marriage. But his wife had made it clear that he didn't make the cut when it came to taking care of her emotional needs.

"The cafeteria is this way."

She fell into step beside him, keeping up with him with ease. His wife had been shorter than him by far, whereas Mysti was taller than Kandid, long-limbed and lithe and...

No. Don't compare them.

"I didn't realize you worked here, too, Jesse."

"I have hospital privileges, but technically, I don't work for Serenity Regional. I have a practice in the building attached to the hospital. And of course I'm called when the hospital gets a patient they need help with." He glanced at her, turning down the corridor where the cafeteria was. "I take it you're going to be working here, then?"

Her brows went up. "Is there any reason why I shouldn't? I was an army surgeon. We're doctors as well."

"I didn't mean that." Was it his imagination or was her level of defensiveness way above where it should have been? "I didn't realize you were out of the military."

"Yes. I'm out." The inflection behind the

words was different than he'd expected. There was a flatness to the tone that went along with her stiff manner. Almost robotic, he would have said.

She was different. In so many ways. But maybe that would work to his benefit. There was no hint that any past attraction from that night in his car had lingered until now.

And on his side?

That hard thud of his gut when he'd seen her said otherwise. But it was manageable, just like the rest of his life. Maybe he should have enlisted as well. He'd found that being regimented helped him stay grounded and comfortable—the impulsiveness from his youth firmly quashed. He was pretty sure that aspect of his nature was good and dead by now. But the side effect of that particular medicine was that he'd ended up being just as regimented at home. He'd never found the switch to turn it off. A point that had caused terrible friction between him and Kandid.

"Well, here it is." He turned into the hospital's small but busy cafeteria. "I can't claim that it's up to gourmet standards, but it does what it needs to do."

The first hint of a genuine smile appeared on her face. "I wouldn't know what to do with it if it were gourmet, so that suits me fine."

Of course. She'd been in the military. She was used to food that was plain and ungarnished.

They got their plates, with Jesse opting for a BLT and fries. Mysti picked up a yogurt and fruit.

She was still very beautiful. Her strawberry blond hair was quite a bit longer than it had been during high school. The shining waves were caught up in a long ponytail that bobbed between her shoulder blades. The freckles across her cheeks and nose were still in evidence, although in school, she'd tried to cover them with makeup. It looked like those days were long gone. There were slight shadows under her eyes that hadn't been there when he'd known her before, either.

They found a small table against a wall and sat down. Mysti wasted no time peeling the top off her yogurt and dipping her spoon into the container. She slid it into her mouth, eyes closing briefly as if savoring the taste.

His head buzzed, and he had a hard time pulling his eyes away from the look of pleasure on her face. Taking a deep breath, he met her gaze, deciding to spear the topic he'd been avoiding. "So what brings you back to Forgotten Point? Or are you? Back, that is."

Maybe she was living on the other side of Serenity in Doak's Cove or even farther out.

Her spoon froze halfway to her mouth before continuing on its path. She finished the movement, the silence lingering while she swallowed.

Just when he thought she wasn't going to answer the question, she shrugged one shoulder. "I am. At least for the next three months. I'm taking Sara Severs's place here while she's on maternity leave. And…well, it seemed like returning home for a while was the logical place to come after leaving the army."

He felt like a jerk for asking the question. But her answer confirmed that her move back wasn't permanent. He should have known it wouldn't be. Felt relieved, actually. She hadn't been able to get out of here fast enough after school, had she? But her mom was here, and it was a natural landing spot since it was someplace familiar with family and people she knew.

"And you, Jesse. You never left town?"

"No. I never did," he said flatly.

Her gaze dipped to his left hand. "How's

Kandid? Did she ever become a teacher like she wanted to in high school?"

The bite of sandwich that he'd taken turned into a rock as it slid down his esophagus. He'd just assumed she'd already known all about Kandid's illness. That her mom would have given her the news. But Kandid herself had rarely mentioned Mysti over the years. He'd wondered if his wife had guessed what happened between him and her friend. But he'd never confessed, and he was pretty sure Mysti had never said anything to anyone, either. It could be they'd simply lost touch, just like he had with some of his old football buddies. Mysti hadn't been at their ten-year high school reunion either, and Jesse had been relieved beyond belief that there'd been no sign of her. Maybe she'd been stationed overseas and hadn't been able to get away.

That made him feel like a clod.

"I thought you knew," he said in a low voice.

Her head tilted. "Knew what?"

"Kandid died three years ago of breast cancer."

There was no sound for several long seconds. Then her voice came through. "Oh,

Jess, I'm so sorry to hear that. I—I didn't know."

Her hand covered his, her expression the softest he'd seen it today. The effect of that look combined with her gentle touch sent a shiver of apprehension through him. What was it about this woman that still got to him so badly? Even after all these years.

"Thank you."

He and Kandid had had a good marriage for the first few years. But by the time Sally was born, they'd begun fighting almost nonstop. And then a year before Kandid's death she'd discovered she had stage IV cancer and the arguments had stopped as quickly as they'd started. Their last year together had been spent fighting the disease, rather than each other, and trying their best to make sure their daughter was spared the worst of the effects of the chemo Kandid had elected to try.

Sally had been only four when her mom had died, and it grieved him how quickly her mother's memories had faded. He kept Kandid's pictures scattered around the house as a way to keep her memory alive.

For Sally's benefit. And his own. Although that thought seemed so hypocritical now, especially sitting across from the one

woman who could have derailed his relationship for good. All it would have taken
was for Mysti to have made one phone call
to Kandid telling her what had happened.
And she would have had every right to tell
on him. But she'd evidently kept her word
and hadn't said anything, because Kandid
had never even hinted that she knew.

And although he'd loved Kandid when
he'd proposed to her—or at least thought
he did at the time—somewhere along the
line, he'd finally admitted to himself that
his rush to the altar had been partially to
assuage his guilt over what had happened
with Mysti. To prove to himself that he was
as far from being like his father as he possi-
bly could be. It hadn't been a good move for
either himself or Kandid. Oh, it had seemed
ridiculously romantic to her at the time that
he couldn't wait to marry her. But his head
hadn't been in the right place, and he'd
walled off parts of himself that she should
have had access to.

Yet despite his mistakes, something truly
good had come of their union. Sally.

He wouldn't trade her for the world.

As if realizing she was still gripping his
hand, Mysti sat back, letting her hands drop
back into her lap.

"I'm surprised your mom didn't tell you," he said evenly.

"Mom always tried to protect me from things she thought might upset me." She stared at her plate. "But you can't always protect people from everything, can you?"

That was the truth. He would have given anything to have been able to shield Kandid from the horrible effects of chemo, would have given anything to protect his daughter from the loss of her mother. But life didn't always work that way. You had to play the cards you were dealt. Unlike a game, though, there was no discarding these cards or trading them for others that had better options.

He'd played them to the best of his ability, although it hadn't always been easy. He was actually grateful Mysti had left, although that had come with its own dose of guilt. Had that last push to leave been because of him? It wasn't like she'd tried to seduce him or anything. The fault in that kiss had been all his. He'd initiated it, and although she'd clung to him like she never wanted to let go, the blame was his alone.

"You're right. You can't." Like Kandid, Jesse hadn't been able to protect Mysti from his impulsive move.

Her chest rose as she sucked down a deep

breath. "So you said you have an office in this building. What do you specialize in?"

The question surprised him. "Geriatrics, actually."

"Really? And you have enough patients to fill a practice?"

He bristled, and he wasn't sure why. "I'm also an internal medicine doctor." His jaw clenched and he tried again. "I see patients other than just those who are up there in years. But my main love is in helping patients who are often brushed aside or not heard the way they should be."

"Sorry, I wasn't trying to offend you. It just took me by surprise, that's all. I knew geriatrics was a specialty, but I've just never met anyone in that branch of medicine." She smiled. "Of course, that could be due to the fact that most soldiers don't use walkers."

Of course it was. If he had thought through her question for a minute, rather than reacting so quickly, he would have realized why she'd never met a geriatrician before.

"Hell, Mysti, I know you weren't trying to offend me. And you didn't. I've just had that same question tossed at me time and time again. And there aren't a ton of us around. If someone wants to go into geriatrics for the money, they've chosen poorly. But if they're in it because they want to help an increasingly vulnerable sector of our population, then I think it can be one of the most rewarding specialties out there."

"Yes. I can understand that. I think I went into surgery for the same reason. I felt I was helping soldiers who were at their most vulnerable. And it was hard, never knowing if someone was going to rally and live or just slip away."

He nodded. "Yes, that's it, exactly."

They looked at each other for a long minute, then Mysti piled her trash onto her tray. "Well, I'm sure you have patients to see this afternoon, so I won't hold you up."

"When do you start work?"

"Tomorrow, actually."

Tomorrow. Even though he had his own office, he ventured into the hospital almost daily due to patients of his who'd been admitted or for administrative reasons. He would be running into her on a regular basis, more than likely, something he'd never in his worst nightmares imagined possible. Hell, it was just one more thing he had to deal with in an already hectic life.

But maybe…

His gaze dipped to her left hand, hoping to see some kind of sign that she was already involved with someone. Or better yet, married. Totally unavailable. But the all-important finger was bare.

That still didn't necessarily mean anything, though, and he certainly didn't want to come out and ask her if she was dating or in a committed relationship.

So he decided to leave things where they were. "You sure you don't want me to show you around?"

"I think I've seen all I need to see."

A hint of relief went through him. At least they would be able to cut this meeting short. And he might make it a point to eat somewhere other than the cafeteria from now on.

If he did that, he could hopefully mitigate any problems that came with seeing her on a regular basis while she was here.

At least that was his hope. But as he'd learned from hard experience, life didn't always hand you what you expected it to.

CHAPTER TWO

MYSTI CAME IN the next day and found a full surgical schedule waiting for her, including one patient whose chart listed Jesse as his personal physician. Not what she needed today. Or any day, really. The shock of seeing him yesterday had thrown her for a loop, even though she'd known that was going to be part of the price of coming back home.

So much for thinking she could just cruise through the next three months with no speed bumps.

She'd hoped it would be a place where she could quietly heal. Instead it threatened to open up old wounds and reignite a guilt that had never entirely gone away.

The scars on her back pulled as she bent over to retrieve a piece of paper that had fallen out of her pocket. She glanced at it. Her mom's grocery list.

Somehow Mysti had thought she might

spot Jesse or Kandid in front of the milk case in the town's small store and steer clear of them until she'd figured out how best to approach seeing them again. She'd half hoped she might not even recognize them after fifteen years and vice versa. But what she hadn't expected was to find that Kandid was no longer alive and that Jesse was a fixture at the hospital.

And she'd recognized him immediately. God, had she ever. And it had brought back a whole host of emotions from a time in her life when she'd felt safe. Safe…except for that one moment when her emotions had gotten the best of her and she'd played with fire.

A good friend's fire.

Jesse hadn't been hers, no matter how much she might have wished it to be different. And there was no way she'd wanted to be the reason he'd broken it off with Kandid. Her decision to leave town had been the correct one. Because he'd gone on to marry his girlfriend. So she'd chalked up what had happened in the car to her long-simmering crush, and the romantic atmosphere created by the close space, the heart-to-heart talk and the storm. They'd been safe in their little cocoon, his voice lulling her into the mystical realm of fairy tales.

She should have known. Fairy tales had never been something that landed on her doorstep. Instead, she'd made choices that had proved devastating. If she hadn't kissed him that night, she might have changed her mind about enlisting. Might not have been accompanying an army friend whose unexpected pregnancy had needed to be kept hidden. Might not have been in the wrong place at the wrong time and had to watch her friend Laura die after triggering an IED and been caught in the blast herself.

Laura's secret had followed her to the grave. And Mysti would have given anything to be able to change the past and go to tell someone about the pregnancy instead of agreeing to her friend's request to stay silent. If she had, Laura might have been shipped home alive. Rather than in a box.

Every time she did surgery, that patchwork of scars on her own back—a stark reminder of what terrible things secrets could do—stretched and ached, not allowing her to forget what had happened and her own responsibility for it. Not that she ever could, even if she wanted to. And she didn't. It somehow seemed fitting that she hadn't come away from the event physically unscathed, no matter what the military psychiatrist had said.

She shook her head to clear it and headed toward the room where Jesse's patient was waiting for her. Seventy-year-old Larry Rogers had a bowel obstruction. The MRIs showed it was scar tissue from a past surgery that had encircled his intestines, slowly strangling a section of it. The surgery should be pretty straightforward.

She went into the exam room and swallowed, her heart sinking.

Straightforward. But not with Jesse standing in the room talking to her patient. Geriatrics. Of course. This had to be the patient who'd listed Jesse as his primary-care doctor She shook her head, frustrated with herself for not remembering. Ugh!

He glanced up and saw her, never missing a beat in what he had been saying to the elderly man. Something about fishing.

Realizing she was frozen in place, she shoved herself forward, forcing her lips to curve in the semblance of a smile. She kept her eyes on her patient. "Hello, Mr. Rogers. I'll be performing your surgery this morning."

The man frowned. "What happened to that other woman? Did you scare her off?"

Her smile faltered, and it was a second before she could engage her tongue to answer him. "Other woman? Oh, you mean Dr. Severs. I'm taking her place while she's on maternity leave." A burst of relief went through her. Who else would the man have meant? Kandid?

Her gaze flitted to Jesse, and she saw his face had transformed, white lines appearing at the sides of his mouth and a dark frown between his brows.

Had his thoughts gone where hers had? Surely not.

"Larry is worried about an upcoming fishing tournament. And how soon he'll be back on his feet," Jesse remarked.

"When is the tournament?" Looking at the man's face, she saw a sad expectancy in it. He didn't expect to survive this surgery. She'd seen the same look on gravely wounded soldiers' faces when the outcome was uncertain.

"In four weeks."

She did some quick calculations. Bowel obstruction surgery could carry up to a three-month recovery period, but since this wasn't a full obstruction and she was doing it laparoscopically, there was hope that by simply cutting through the fibrous scar tissue, it would free the intestines to start functioning normally again. Although anything could happen. She could get in there and find a situation that was more complicated than the MRI showed.

She touched his arm. "We'll see what we can do. Will you have someone in the boat with you? Or is this a solo competition?"

"No, we'll fish in pairs. I've always partnered with my son. I've fished this tournament for over thirty years."

A pang went through her. She remembered fishing in it with her dad. It was one of the things she'd missed while she'd been stationed in Joronha. And now her father was gone. There'd be no fishing with him ever again. So she could guess how important this tournament was for both Larry and his son.

She tilted her head. "If he can do most of the heavy lifting, I don't see any reason why you wouldn't be able to go." The tournaments in Forgotten Point weren't fly-fishing, where his arm and abs would be in constant motion, aggravating his surgical site.

"Maybe I'll even enter the tournament, so I can keep an eye on you."

Jesse's head whipped around to look at her, but he didn't say anything.

"Who would your partner be?" Mr. Rogers asked curiously.

The pang in her belly sharpened. "I'm sure I can find someone. I used to enter with my dad, but…" The rest of her sentence got caught in her throat.

"Which is why I don't want to miss this with my son. None of us knows how long we'll travel this earth."

Damn, she needed to derail this conversation quickly. "Well, you'll be traveling this earth for a while longer, I think. So let me get to work and see about getting those insides of yours free and working again."

For the first time since she'd entered the room, the older man smiled. "Let's get to it, then."

Their patient had already signed forms giving her permission to operate, and although those papers outlined the risks, she hoped everything would go smoothly.

Except why on earth had she said she might enter the tournament?

Because the look on his face had spoken

volumes. And in some part of her, Mysti still felt she had some sort of penance to pay.

So much for all those months of therapy. Snap your fingers and you could regress all the way back to the beginning.

She finally forced herself to glance again at Jesse. "Do you want me to let you know when the surgery is done?"

"Not necessary. I'll know. Because I'll be there."

Shock held her still for a moment. He was planning on coming into the operating room with her? There was no way she'd agree to that. As if he knew she was about to cry foul, though, he added, "I'll be in the observation room."

Okay, so that was almost worse than him being in the actual room with them. She was still getting her feet back on the ground. She was used to having back-to-back cases of trauma surgery, where she had to work as fast as she could to save lives. The space between patients here at the hospital seemed so huge. So organized.

"You don't have other patients to see?" she asked him slightly desperately.

"Not until this afternoon."

Didn't he trust her with his patient?

Hell, why should he? They didn't know each other. Not anymore.

Actually, they hadn't known each other back then, either, despite living next door to each other. Not properly. They'd only been kids.

It was on the tip of her tongue to bite out a sharp reply, but she didn't want Mr. Rogers wondering what was going on between them. Because nothing was.

"Okay. I guess I'll see you after the surgery, then."

Mr. Rogers smiled at her. "And I'll expect to see you in a boat in four weeks' time. I'll have you know my son and I have won the last two years."

"Then I'll have to see if I can give you some stiff competition this year, won't I?"

With that, she smiled one last time, hoping and praying that the glass to the observation room was one way and that she wouldn't see him up there. Serenity Regional wasn't a teaching hospital; it was a small local medical center that she remembered from her own childhood and adolescence. But she'd never actually thought she'd be on this side of the patient-doctor equation.

Was this where Kandid had died? Not a

question she was ever going to ask anyone. And the sooner she got out of here and completed this surgery, the sooner she would be rid of Mr. Rogers's primary doctor, too.

At least for today. Suddenly the thought of three months working in such close proximity to Jesse seemed to stretch ahead of her like a never-ending road. All she could do was take it one day at a time, and hope like hell she made it through.

Mysti's glorious hair was nowhere in sight, having been ruthlessly stuffed into a surgical cap. But that didn't mean Jesse couldn't immediately pick her out of the team. Her high cheekbones and delicately arched brows were somehow burned into his memory. He immediately tried to call up Kandid's image and found it more than a little blurry after three years. Except it had been a hell of a lot longer than three years since he'd seen Mysti.

His gut clenched as guilt arced through his system, just as sharp today as it had been fifteen years ago. He flicked it away with an angry sweep of a mental broom. This was ridiculous.

It wasn't like he had sat around pining

after Mysti for all these years. No, he'd lived his life with the knowledge that she was out of his life forever.

Except here she was, back again. For now.

Surgery was well under way. She'd said she expected it to take around an hour to free the intestines.

She made her first small incision and then another one after that. She was hoping everything could be done laparoscopically unless she ran into a complication. Her fingers fed the scope and her instruments through the incisions and like magic, the screen at the front of the room lit up, magnifying what was happening inside his patient's body. Her eyes were also focused on the screen and Jesse had the sensation that they were looking at this together, his mind running through the steps that would happen, even though he wasn't a surgeon. As long as Mr. Rogers remained stable and she didn't nick something other than the scar tissue while in there, she was right—it would be a fairly easy surgery.

Once she was past the muscle, the smooth, pale structure of his intestines came into view. Mysti had already mapped out the location of the adhesion, which was fortunately not all the way at the bottom of the stack. She moved the scope farther in and the problem area immediately came into sight. The squeezed section of intestine was red and angry-looking. The tissue encircling it was thankfully not so thin that it had actually cut through the organ. Instead it was thick and fibrous-looking.

"I'm at the area of adhesion. Going to cut through both sides and pull the tissue out to keep it from wrapping back around."

She skillfully moved the other instruments, using one to grip and cut and then held it while she moved to the other side and snipped that as well. Her glance went toward where he sat, but there was no way she could see him from her side since the glass was actually made like a mirror. He was glad. Something about her eyes meeting his still had this incredibly weird effect on him.

And the fact that she was willing to go out on a boat and fish near her patient just to make sure he was okay? That sounded like something *he* would do. Jesse tended to show he cared for someone in practical ways. Kandid had had a hard time understanding that. And it had been partly to blame for the rift that grew between them. That in itself was probably responsible for what had happened later in their marriage. The funny thing was in the end it hadn't been him who'd been unfaithful. It had been Kandid.

He turned his mind back to the tournament.

Who would Mysti pair up with? He blinked. Did she even have access to a boat?

A thought swirled in his head, which he discarded before taking it right back up again. It wouldn't hurt to ask what her plans were. If she'd just been saying she'd go fishing without really meaning it, Larry would be horribly disappointed. Maybe Jesse could take Sally out on the lake and fish nearby for the same reason that Mysti had said she was going. He hadn't been out on the lake in ages. Larry was right. None of them knew how long they'd get to travel on this earth. And Sally was growing up far too quickly. Life had been kind of in limbo since Kandid had passed away. They'd bought the boat to use as a family, but Kandid had been diagnosed with cancer soon afterward so it was virtually new. Maybe it was high time he got it out of the storage area and checked if it still floated.

He might not have been the ideal husband, but he was determined to be a good dad.

The kind of dad he hadn't had when he was a kid.

When his head cleared a little, he glanced down to see that Mysti had completed Larry's surgery and was saying something out of range of the microphone to the anesthesiologist. That was his signal to get moving and head down toward the recovery room. She couldn't see him anyway, so any kind of congratulatory signal would be hidden behind the one-way glass.

Soon he was in one of the rooms, and Larry's gurney arrived a minute or so later. His patient was already awake, although he was pretty groggy. Jesse moved toward the bed just as Mysti came into the room. She'd already stripped off her PPE, except for her hat and booties.

Jesse smiled at her. "Congratulations. It looked like everything went well."

"So you were in there, watching."

"Of course." Did she not think he'd keep his word?

Her eyes moved to take in Larry as well. "Hi. I found that pesky scar tissue that was causing the problem. You should start feeling better very soon, once the soreness from the procedure wears off."

Larry struggled to focus. "I'll be okay?"

"More than okay." Mysti squeezed his arm, leaning over the bed. "I'm thinking you're definitely going to make your fishing tournament in four weeks' time."

"Good." The man's voice was slightly raspy from being intubated. "You're still coming, right?"

"I'll be there... Somehow." Her voice had lowered so that Jesse could barely hear her last word.

Was she already regretting making Larry that promise? Or maybe he'd been right, and she didn't have a boat.

Something that was easy enough to find out. "Larry, I'll be back to check on you this afternoon before I leave, okay?"

The man gave him a weak thumbs-up sign.

Jesse then turned to Mysti. "Could I see you outside for a minute?" He held open the door.

Her eyes widened before she nodded and walked through it. "Sure. I have about a half hour before my next surgery."

"How many more do you have scheduled today?" He frowned. Hopefully Serenity Regional wouldn't work her into the ground on her first day.

She's a big girl, Jess. She can handle herself.

"Just one. I know my limits." She gave a half shrug and a smile. "Most of the time, anyway."

Was she saying he didn't know his? Like on that stormy night fifteen years ago when he'd stepped over a line he never should have crossed?

That was one conversation he wasn't planning on having. Now or ever. So he steered back to the topic at hand. "Larry really looks forward to those fishing tournaments."

She frowned. "I know he does. I grew up here, too, remember?"

Tension wound in his skull. "Except you haven't been home in years. So it's hard for you to know just how important this is for him, specifically." He hadn't seen her once since that day they'd gotten caught in the storm.

Her chin went up. "I'm aware of how often I came home. My parents regularly used their vacation time to come and see me, whenever I wasn't stationed outside the country." She paused. "I'm not sure what you're getting at, Jess."

Every time she said the informal, shortened version of his name like that, as she'd done when they were young, it elicited a muscular reaction in him. A tightening of abs that he hoped she couldn't see. He forged forward. "You told him you would come out on the water and keep an eye on him. He'll be expecting you to do just that, if nothing more than to have people around him."

Her eyes shut for a split second. "I know, and as soon as I said it I realized I shouldn't have. I was trying to make sure he was as stress-free as possible before surgery."

"So you lied." He thrust down a feeling of disappointment.

"No!" She looked down at her hands. "My dad and I used to go every year, too, before I enlisted. I just…it'll be hard to be out there alone. With all of those memories of how it used to be when I was with him."

He knew what she meant. But it had nothing to do with fishing. Jesse and his father had not been close and had never done things together like fishing tournaments. Or anything, really. His dad had been way too busy trying to prove his virility with anything that moved.

Hell. He hadn't brought her out here to go down these old roads yet again.

Before he could think of a response, though, she continued in a soft voice. "Besides, Mom sold the boat a couple of years ago to someone in Forgotten Point."

That's what he thought. "I have a boat."

"Oh, I couldn't borrow—"

"No, not borrow. But maybe we could go out and fish in that tournament together, so that you don't disappoint Larry. Like he said, it has to be done in pairs at least, so you can't fish alone. And it wouldn't be safe. I'm sure Sally would be ecstatic to come along, too."

Mysti visibly recoiled, her eyes wide with a look of horror. Was the thought of fishing with him that abhorrent? Hell, why wouldn't it be? He'd kissed her while still dating Kandid. Did he really expect her to let that go? To allow them to go back to being friends?

"I wouldn't want to intrude on you and your…friend."

"Friend? What friend?" He had no idea what she was talking about.

"This Sally person. Although after Kandid, I'm glad you've been able to find…"

Her voice faded away as if she didn't want to finish her thought. He realized in a second what she thought, and he laughed. A short sound that was born of relief, not mirth. Was that why she'd flinched? She thought he was involved with someone else. His laughter died a hard death. So she thought he was inviting her out on the lake while involved with someone else?

"Sally isn't a friend or a girlfriend, Myst." He swallowed a hard lump in his throat before pushing the next words out. "She's my daughter."

CHAPTER THREE

FOR A SECOND or two no one said anything.

Jesse had a daughter? With Kandid? Her mom had never mentioned it. Then again, why would she feel the need to detail every birth in Forgotten Point? Especially when it had to do with Jesse. Neither her mom nor Kandid knew what had happened in that car between her and Jesse, but Mysti was pretty sure her mom had guessed something had gone on between them. It made her doubly glad she'd left town so soon afterward. If Kandid had ever found out...

Well, Jesse might not have his daughter.

"I—I'm sorry. I didn't know you had children."

"Child. One child. Sally. She was only four when Kandid passed away."

"I'm so sorry. I can't imagine how difficult that was." Her dad had died of a heart attack while she was in Joronha. At the time, there'd been few flights out and despite bending over backward, she hadn't been able to come home for the funeral. It had made what happened to Laura that much harder. Because her remains had been shipped home, and Mysti hadn't been able to be there for that funeral, either.

"It wasn't a fun time, that's for sure." He pulled his phone out and glanced at it. "I know you have your next surgery coming up. So about the fishing tournament? Will you come with Sally and me? Or should I just take your place as Larry's babysitter?" He said it with a smile as if trying to soften the question.

So you lied?

His earlier words whispered through her mind. Unfortunately, when it came to Jesse she'd lied about more than that one thing. She'd lied about her feelings for him back in that car. She hadn't lied about visiting the recruiter. But she'd lied about Forgotten Point making her feel claustrophobic. Had lied about itching to see the world and shaking the town's dust off her feet. But if she hadn't…

Suddenly she wanted to meet his daughter. Needed to see the child that he'd had with someone else. Maybe that would finally drive home the fact that he'd loved someone else back then. Loved that person enough to marry her and have a child with her. And since Sally would be…what… seven, now, it wasn't like Kandid had gotten pregnant while dating Jesse and had a rushed wedding. They'd *wanted* to get married. Had loved each other enough to commit to each other for life. And hopefully Jesse had proved to himself once and for all that he wasn't like his dad, since it sounded like he and Kandid had kept their vows, including 'til death do you part.

"Yes, I'll come. If you're sure Sally won't mind."

"No, she won't. I'd thought of selling my boat actually, too."

She understood that. Had understood her mom's reasons for not wanting to hold on to something that brought back painful memories of happier times. But maybe having a daughter helped Jesse with the pain of Kandid's loss.

"I'm glad you have her, Jess. Sally, that is." The soft words came out of nowhere, but she wouldn't take them back, even if she could.

"Thank you. She's my whole world." He

smiled and glanced at her. "Hey, do you have time for a coffee before your next case?"

Something about the way he was looking at her sent a shiver of remembrance over her. God, when he'd stared at her in the car that night, she'd been completely lost. Had forgotten about everything except for being there with him. And right now, her thoughts were shifting in that direction.

No. Not again.

She could not afford to be caught off guard again. Couldn't afford to let him get close only to have him pull back from her in horror like he'd done in that car.

Straightening her spine, she gave him a direct look. "I... If we could keep things on a professional level, I think the next three months will be easier on both of us."

Lord, he hadn't been asking her out on a date. Just coffee. But she'd made it sound like he was making a play for her, her own self-righteous little speech making her wince. "I'm sorry, Jesse, I didn't mean that the way it came out."

But it was too late. The softness in his face had disappeared. "It's okay. You're right—thanks for that piece of advice. It's not like we grew up next door to each other or anything." His head tilted. "What happened to you, Mysti, that a simple offer of coffee has you suddenly bristling with the need to remind me that you're getting out of Forgotten Point—again—just as soon as you can?"

A crushing sense of regret flattened her. He was right. They'd practically grown up together. So her comment about keeping things on a professional level had to have been a slap in the face. Little did he know that it had come out of a need to protect her heart. Out of the fear that she might find her feelings for him weren't quite so dead after all.

Well, good. Maybe it was better for him to think she was cold and unfeeling. He had no idea just how cold she could be.

"What happened to me, Jesse? Wow. That's rich coming from someone who's never stepped foot outside of their own little world." She was digging herself in deeper, but the words kept pouring out no matter how hard she tried to stop them. "I had to change in order to survive army life—to cope with what I saw on a daily basis. Soldiers who were little more than children came across my table one after the other. Some with missing limbs. Some who were too far gone to save. If I let myself feel too much, I couldn't have done my job."

She swallowed back what felt like a solid ball of emotion. "Once again, I am so sorry, Jess. You didn't deserve to have me unload on you like that. The transition from the military to civilian life has been harder than I expected, although that doesn't excuse it." She clasped her hands in front of her, fingers biting into each other. "You'll let me know about the tournament?"

"You sure you still want to go?"

His tone was tight and rough. Evidently she wasn't forgiven. Although why would he? She'd been a witch with a capital *B*.

"I want to help Larry, although I'll completely understand if you no longer want to let me on your boat."

"You're welcome to come. We'll just draw a line down the middle and each keep to our own sides."

She shot him a quick glance, not entirely sure if he was joking or serious, but there was no way she was going to ask. "Thank you. I'll make sure to clear my schedule."

"I'll check on Larry this afternoon. I can just text you a report, if you're too busy to make it back to see him."

"That would be great. I'll try to check

in on him, but it depends on how my day goes," she said.

He nodded, pausing for a second or two. "This must all seem incredibly boring after your army work."

It wasn't. But that didn't mean it was any easier. Maybe coming back to Forgotten Point had been a huge mistake.

"Right now, boring is good. Very good. Because it means people aren't dying." She glanced at the clean white walls and floors that were so different from her work in medical tents. At least gunfire couldn't easily penetrate these walls. When snatches of the more disturbing memories started infiltrating her head, she knew it was time to go. Before they had a chance to take over. Or before she snapped at Jesse again for no good reason whatsoever. "Let me know about Larry, okay? I do need to go."

"Yes, of course. Go. I'll see you later."

Yes, he would. And that was part of the problem. But like what she'd seen in Joronha, she would just have to somehow compartmentalize Jesse and not let him take over her thoughts.

And hopefully with the boundaries she'd just set for herself and for him, she'd be able to succeed in that goal.

* * *

The rest of her day was uneventful, thankfully. The surgery she'd had scheduled after Larry's was to clean out an infected pocket in someone's leg. It had taken all of thirty minutes. Found deep in the patient's thigh, the fact that it had become encapsulated had both helped and hurt treatment. While it had kept the infection from spreading to nearby tissues and from eroding the large blood vessel that it was pressed against, those things had provided challenges in not nicking said vessel. And it had also been why it had been hard for antibiotics to push into the cocoon of infection.

She was just finishing up her paperwork when one of the nurses told her someone was waiting for her at the information desk. Her muscles tensed instantly before she forced them to relax. It wasn't Jesse.

Not that she'd wanted it to be.

She glanced at her phone to see if she'd had any calls and saw that she'd missed two from her mom. A trickle of fear went through her. Heading for the elevator, she pressed the call button, hoping it was nothing serious.

Her mother answered immediately. "Hi, honey, I was just wondering if you're still up to going with me to pick up Brutus. I know you said you were getting off around five."

Oh, hell, she'd completely forgotten. Fortunately, she was done for the day.

"Are you downstairs? I'm headed there now."

"Yes, I thought I'd just come and wait since the vet is on this side of the bridge."

Brutus was her parents' dog. Well, he'd actually been her dad's pride and joy. And although her mother loved the Saint Bernard dearly, he was quite a chunker—especially if he had to be lifted into the car. Much like the patient she'd just had, Brutus had gotten himself speared by a branch he'd been tossing around. It had lodged, then broken off in the dog's left thigh. Trying to lift his bulk into the car to go to the vet's had taken both of them, with her mom inside guiding the front and Mysti lifting from the back, while trying to hurt the pup as little as possible.

"How's he doing?"

"They said he's sore. I'm sure someone at the office could help me get him into the car, if you're busy."

"Nope. I'm just finishing up. See you in a minute."

But by the time she stepped off the elevator five minutes later, she saw that her mom was not alone. Jesse was there talking to her.

She tensed, then relaxed. It was what people did here. They engaged in small talk. All the time. He wasn't telling her about their fishing plans. Not that they were plans. And even if he was, what did it matter? It wasn't like it was a date or anything.

Maybe she was afraid her mom would take it that way. After all, Jesse was an eligible widower. And her mom had always liked him when they were kids.

It's not like we grew up next door to each other or anything.

Those words were going to haunt her for a long time.

But they weren't kids anymore, and her mom had already made vague hints about the grandchildren she hoped to have one day. And since Mysti was an only child, nobody else but her could bestow that pleasure on her mother.

Mysti knew she did want children. She'd just never found anyone to "want" them with. Her glance strayed to Jesse before popping away in a rush.

She hurried over to them. "Hey."

Jesse nodded to her. "Hi. I was just getting ready to go check on Larry. I finished up later than I thought I would."

"Actually, I did make it up there. He's doing fine."

Her mom looked from one to the other. "Larry Rogers? Was his surgery today?"

Another thing about small towns was that everyone knew practically everything about the other folks who lived there. It was pretty amazing that her mom had never found out about her and Jesse's kiss all those years ago. But the only people who'd known they were in that car together were Mysti, Jesse and the officer who'd stopped to make sure they were okay. And he'd clearly had no clue about what he'd interrupted.

Thank God he'd come along when he had, though.

"It was." Even though it was her mom, she still needed to respect the HIPAA laws.

"I don't suppose you can tell me how he is other than what you just said to Jesse?" Her mom waved off the question. "I know. It's okay. I'm sure someone in town knows every detail of that surgery by now."

Mysti laughed. It was true. HIPAA was no match for the town's robust rumor mill. She glanced at Jesse. "Well, we're off to pick up Brutus from the vet. Our dog," she added, in case he didn't know who she was talking about.

"I've seen Brutus out in the front yard when I've driven by the house. Is he okay? Or is that protected under HIPAA, too?"

Mysti laughed, glad for the lighter atmosphere between them. "He's doing fine. He speared himself with part of a tree and had to have surgery, but it looks like they got him all fixed up."

"Do you need me to lend a hand?"

Mysti's "Oh, no!" was countered with, "Oh, could you?" by her mom. She shot her a glance, but her mother just smiled.

"You know how hard it was for us to hoist him in by ourselves when we drove to the vet."

"But we managed, right?" There was a hint of desperation behind the words, but if her mom heard it, she was clever enough to ignore it.

"Which vet is it?" Jesse asked.

Her mom answered. "Bowman's. Just before you go over the bridge into Forgotten Point."

Leave it to her mom to point out that it would be on Jesse's way home.

"Tell you what," Jesse said, "I'll follow you over in my car. That'll be just about the time I normally pick Sally up from the aftercare program at school. And since you told me Larry is doing okay, I'll take your word for it."

Mysti gave an internal sigh. "If you're sure."

"I am."

Like a little caravan, the three vehicles made the trek to the vet's office and walked in together. As soon as her mom spoke to the woman at the reception desk, the sound of howling came from somewhere in the back. Brutus must have heard her mom's voice.

The receptionist smiled. "Can you tell he's been waiting for you? Every time the bell on the door rings he howls, despite still being under the influence of anesthesia." She sized Jesse up. "Good thing you brought help. He's not the steadiest on his feet right now. I'll let them know you're here."

A few minutes later, the Saint Bernard, wearing a massive cone around his neck, came through the door, his nails clicking and bumping as he struggled to pull his handler forward.

Then he was at her mom's side whining and shaking his head, as if trying to rid himself of the protective contraption.

Jesse stepped forward and took the leash, giving the dog a pat on his shoulder.

The vet tech said, "His leg isn't bandaged because of where the wound was, so the cone needs to stay on for a few days to keep him from messing with his stitches. Can you bring him back in a week? His leg should be less sore by then, so he should be back to being able to jump in the car." She eyed the group. "So you won't need a sling and hoist to lift him into it."

Her mom nodded. "That will be good. My husband was always great with that." Her eyes moistened for a second before she cleared her throat, as if chasing the emotion away.

Mysti's heart clenched. She remembered her mom letting her know that her father had a new puppy and that he was going to be a whopper. She was sure neither of them had any idea that her mom would be managing Brutus alone someday. She glanced at Jesse. "Want me to take him?"

"Nope, we're fine, aren't we, boy?"

In answer, Brutus sat on the tile flooring whining, his tail thumping on the ground.

She couldn't help but smile. It hadn't taken long for Jesse to win the dog over. Then again, it hadn't taken him any time at all to win Mysti over, either. She'd always been a sucker for the man's smile and long dark eyelashes. That certainly hadn't changed. Although she really wished it had.

Her mom thanked the receptionist and waited as Jesse and Brutus went through the door and headed out to her car.

"Back seat, I'm assuming?" he called over his shoulder.

"Yes, please. Passenger side. I have a blanket laid out for him already." Her mom took out her keys and pressed the unlock button on the fob.

Mysti went to the door on the opposite side, so she could help guide him, but before she could even get in place, Jesse had his door opened and Brutus put his front feet on the seat.

"Okay, boy, here we go." Sliding one arm under the pup's belly and the other behind his back legs, he lifted the dog with seeming ease, making the heaving and ho-ing she and her mom had done earlier seem like a joke. Brutus didn't even whimper.

"They must have given him some pretty strong meds." Mysti couldn't help the slight waspishness in her voice. Why did he make everything he did look so effortless?

Like letting her walk away from him that night fifteen years ago?

No, he'd done the right thing there. And Mysti had gone out of her way to make sure he was free to go back to Kandid by leaving town.

Ha! Had her motivations really been that selfless? Or had she not been able to stand the thought of seeing him with one of her closest friends?

Either way, she'd felt there had been no choice. At the time, anyway.

And now?

They'd both moved on with their lives. And Jesse had a daughter. So whatever romanticized feelings she might still have about that night were meaningless. He'd loved Kandid. Had married her and had a child with her. Crucially, he had also not even tried to talk Mysti out of leaving Forgotten Point.

So that was that. She needed to do what he had done and get on with her life.

After Laura had died from that IED blast, Mysti had used all kinds of coping mechanisms to help herself get through her grief. But none of it had erased the horror and tragedy of that day. Her counselor had warned her against trying to mask the pain with drugs, alcohol, or damaging relationships. He'd told her the best thing to do was to face the pain and acknowledge it. Then to move forward.

She was still a little shaky on the last part of that equation, but she was trying to learn.

"Okay, Mom, I'll see you at the house." She forced herself to add, "Thanks for the help, Jesse."

"Happy to do it. Are you sure you don't need me to help you get him back out again?"

"No, he can pretty much do a marine crawl and then slide out on his own."

With a wave, her mom got into the car and headed on her way.

Mysti hesitated for a minute, glancing at him. "Well, I'd better go so I can help her."

"Right. I'm sure I'll see you around at the hospital."

Unfortunately she was sure that was true. But outside of leaving Forgotten Point before her three months were up, that was inevitable. So she would do what her counselor had said and turn and face the pain and regret of that time and then move forward with her life.

She slid into her vehicle, and with a final wave she turned the key in the ignition. It clicked, but didn't start. Oh God, please no. She tried again, with the same result. The car didn't even try to turn over.

That's what she got for buying the first used car she came across. But it wasn't a clunker, and she'd needed something quickly.

Why oh why did it have to die on her now? In front of Jesse?

Right on cue, he motioned for her to roll down her window. She did, glad the electrical system still worked. "It's okay. I'll just call Triple-A. I think it's just the battery."

"I'll take you to your mom's, if you don't mind making a pit stop by the school. It'll only take a minute or two."

"Thanks, Jesse. Sorry about this."

"Don't be. We all get stranded at some point or another."

Like they had all those years ago during that storm? The thought made her chest hurt.

"Well, thanks. I'll call my mom on the way and ask her to wait for us before trying to get Brutus out."

She collected her belongings and then climbed into Jesse's SUV, which of course started up immediately. Then she called her mom and left her a voice mail saying they were on their way.

Five minutes later they were in front of the school in the pickup lane. It was incongruous that the Jesse she'd known back in high school, football player, accomplished athlete and the guy every girl wanted to date, was now a father, doing ordinary father things.

But he'd also been widowed at a young age, had succeeded in getting through medical school with a wife and a child, whereas Mysti had been unencumbered by romantic ties when she'd been in school. If she had gotten married young, would she have gone through with any of her life goals?

She actually didn't think so. In the end, her leaving had not only been the right thing for Jesse, it had been the right thing for her. For the first time, she could see that with clear eyes.

Her heart lightened a bit. Maybe it had taken coming home again to see that. So as hard as it had been to come face-to-face with her past, she'd done it. Had confronted it head-on and could now move forward. She mentally snipped one of the elastic cords that tied her to the past.

"So your daughter's name is Sally?"

"Yes." He seemed to scan the lines of kids

and teachers who stood waiting in front of the school. "She looks a lot like Kandid."

Of course she did. Mysti's heart squeezed again as she wondered for a brief moment what her own daughter might have looked like if she'd had one.

She thanked God again for that officer stopping by their car all those years ago. Because if he hadn't… Well, life might have gotten a lot more complicated in ways she didn't want to think about. Her actions could have hurt a whole lot of people. Because as she'd learned, actions really did have consequences.

"I'm happy for you, Jess. Not for losing Kandid, obviously, but for the life you've made for yourself here."

"Despite not stepping foot outside of this town?" He coasted forward as the line in front of them shifted before glancing over at her with a smile that took the sting out of the words. "You never married."

"No. But it was a complicated time. Between medical school and being deployed, life was pretty busy." She shifted her left shoulder as remembered pain rippled through her back, the memory of searing-hot shrapnel slicing through her uniform and embedding itself into her skin and muscle.

The car ahead of them moved forward again, and then they were in front of the school and Jesse rolled down his window to tell them who his child was.

And then a little girl came over. An adorable little girl with dark pigtails and huge brown eyes. He was right. She looked like Kandid. But Mysti also saw Jesse in there as a dimple flashed in her cheek.

"Hi, Daddy!"

The happy greeting made Mysti's heart clench.

"Hi, Sal, good day?"

The girl giggled. "The best."

A teacher opened the back door. "Don't forget to tell your dad about mismatch day on Friday." The woman glanced over at Mysti and did a double take. "Mysti North! Long time no see. I didn't realize you were back in town."

The face clicked with a name. Anna. A friend she'd gone to school with. "I am. And of course my car broke down and Jesse was kind enough to give me a lift to my mom's house."

Anna closed the door after Sally got in. "Let me give you my number. Maybe we can go to dinner sometime and catch up. It's really good to see you."

"Thanks, that would be great." Mysti pulled in a deep breath, glad that maybe she could start forging some of those old connections again. She typed the number Anna recited into her phone. "I'll give you a call."

Anna nodded, then backed away from the car so they could pull away.

Looking into his rearview mirror, Jesse addressed his daughter. "So your day was the best?"

"Except for my spelling test, which I think I bombed."

Mysti couldn't suppress a smile as she turned to study the girl. She remembered those days when her biggest fear was bombing a test.

"Sally, this is Mysti North. She's an old friend who just moved back to town."

"Oh, hi! I didn't know my dad had any friends."

Jesse laughed. "Wait a minute. I do have friends."

"Only guy friends, and they don't count. I think it's good for you to have girlfriends, too."

Girlfriends. Yikes!

Mysti's face heated. But it answered her question about any new women that might be in his life. Then again, he probably wouldn't parade just anyone in front of his daughter, unless the relationship was serious.

Wisely, Jesse changed the subject. "So how would you like to go out on the boat in a few weeks and take part in a fishing tournament?"

"Really? That would be cool." Sally seemed to think for a minute. "Would I have to touch worms?"

"Not unless you want to. Mysti will be joining us, if that's okay."

She could feel the child's dark eyes shift from her dad to her. "Yes. We have a really nice boat. But Dad says we don't have time to use it."

A muscle worked in Jesse's jaw. Thinking about how he'd used to boat when Kandid was still alive? Lord. Every time Jesse looked at his daughter, he probably saw his late wife. The ache in her chest grew to encompass the pain he must have gone through when Kandid died. Probably still went through. It had hurt Mysti horribly when Laura died. Not only because she was a close friend, but because of the senseless way in which it had happened.

"Well," Jesse said, glancing in the mirror again, "I'm trying to change that, okay?"

"Yay!" She glanced at Mysti. "Do I have to call you Mrs. North?"

She swallowed. How did you explain to a child that it wasn't *Mrs.*? She turned to Jesse. "Are you okay with her calling me Mysti?"

"That's up to you."

Turning back to the girl, she said. "How about it? Want to just call me Mysti?"

"Misty…is that like fog?"

She laughed. "Something like that."

"I like that name." The child peered closer. "Your eyes are pretty."

"Thank you." She liked his daughter. She was sweet and curious, but not afraid to ask questions or assert her opinion on things.

And if she'd thought Mysti's eyes were ugly, would she still think that?

Jesse turned onto one of the side streets that led to her mom's house. In another minute or two they were there. "Thanks again for the ride." She glanced at Sally. "And it was very nice meeting you."

"I'm glad you're coming to fish with us. And that dad finally has a girlfriend."

Out of the corner of her eye, she saw Jesse roll his eyes, which made her laugh again.

"I'm just a friend." But despite her words, for the first time since Jesse had offered to go fishing with her, Mysti was actually glad she'd agreed.

He asked her if she needed help getting her car, but she shook her head. "We'll get Brutus settled and then my mom can run me back to the vet's office."

"And you're sure you don't need help lifting him out of the car."

"Yes, I'm sure." Her mom was already getting out of her car and opening the door. "And I'd better go or she'll try to do it all on her own. Thanks again, Jess. And I'll see you later, Sally."

With that, she exited the vehicle, and without looking behind her, she headed toward her mom and Brutus.

CHAPTER FOUR

SALLY HAD TALKED nonstop about the fishing trip—and his new "girlfriend," Mysti—ever since she'd found out they would be going. It had taken forever to explain to his daughter the difference between a girl who was a friend and a girlfriend and why Mysti was only the former. It had also sent a warning flare up in his head, and he realized how easily his daughter could attach herself to a mother figure. It was one reason he'd never really dated. Oh, he'd had a couple of quick encounters after being asked out for drinks. But it had felt wrong, knowing his mom was watching his daughter while he rolled around in someone else's bed. So it had been a year since he'd gone out with anyone, for drinks or anything else.

He would not see his daughter hurt. By anyone.

Even if Kandid had lived, he wondered if

their marriage would have lasted. It seemed like the longer they were together, the further apart they had grown. And as much as he tried to tell himself that it was inevitable for couples to find other interests that held their attention as the years went by, he'd sensed something else was going on. Especially when she constantly complained about him being emotionally unavailable.

He'd found out exactly what she meant by that after she'd gotten her diagnosis, confessing that she'd cheated on him with a coworker. She'd cried and promised it was over.

At least she'd confessed. Which was more than what he'd done about Mysti. He'd never told Kandid about that, and it had eaten at him for years. The truth was, he'd felt nothing but relief that he wasn't the only one who'd fallen to temptation. And that worried him on another level entirely. Shouldn't he have been furious with his wife for cheating on him? Angry with the man she'd been with?

Instead he'd found she was right in her assessment of his emotions, or lack thereof. Because he'd felt a complete detachment over her announcement that had startled him, made him realize he'd just been going through the motions with her for years, maybe even since they'd gotten married. Guilt over his own actions with Mysti, perhaps?

He shook his head to clear his thoughts. It didn't matter now. They hadn't divorced, and Kandid had died. The condolences had been hard to get through at the funeral, because he'd felt like such a hypocrite. To the outside world they'd seemed like the perfect couple: high school sweethearts who had lived out their vows until the very end. A fairy tale. Except that's all it had been. Make-believe.

The cell phone on his desk buzzed. He glanced at the readout and frowned. It was the hospital. He'd just been getting ready to leave the office. His mom had Sally for the night after his daughter pleaded that they wanted to watch movies and eat popcorn, since it was a Friday night.

"Dr. Grove here."

"This is Reggie Worth. I'm a nurse in the trauma unit. We have a patient down here who's been involved in a car accident. Her daughter just arrived and says she's a patient of yours."

"Who is it?"

"Helen Hastings."

He'd just seen Helen two hours ago for a routine checkup. She must have had the accident on her way home. "I'll be right down."

Helen was in good health except for osteoporosis. And if she'd been in a traffic accident...

His receptionist promised to lock up the office, so he made his way down to the main hospital. Unlike his office, which had finished seeing patients for the day, Serenity Regional never closed, never slept. It saw patients at all hours of the day and night.

He took the elevator to the second floor and headed to the nurse's desk. "Helen Hastings?"

The nurse glanced at her computer screen. "Room three. The surgeon is with her now."

"Thanks."

Surgeon. So the injuries weren't minor. Hell.

Helen's daughter Dorothy was in the hallway.

"How is she?" he asked.

"I don't know. She's broken several bones and may have internal bleeding."

He squeezed her arm. "I'll check on her."

Pushing through the door, he found Mysti leaning over the bed, palpating Helen's stomach.

He should have known she'd be there.

"What have you got?" he asked.

If she was surprised to see him, she didn't show it. "She was unconscious when she arrived, but from the feel of her belly we've got a possible ruptured spleen. I'm taking her into surgery. She has fractures to both of her femurs and to her left tibia, but those are going to have to wait. Anything on her chart I need to know about?"

"She has osteoporosis, but as far as allergies go, no. It should be on her chart with the hospital."

"It is, but since they said you're her primary care physician, I wanted to double-check."

Two nurses came in and got the IV cords adjusted and then unlocked the bed so they could wheel it down the hallway to the surgical area.

Mysti threw him a glance. "I need to scrub in. If I can get her stable, orthopedics will come in and set the bones."

"Go. I'll sit with her daughter."

In a small town like this, he knew almost everyone, was friends with most of the people who lived there. It made it hard to be completely impartial, and Dorothy had been friends with his mother for many years.

"I'll let you know."

Odds were, Mysti knew the family as well, but she was in surgeon's mode and anxious to see to her patient.

He went back into the hallway and asked Dorothy to join him in the waiting room, checking to see if she wanted a cup of coffee or some water.

"No, nothing right now. What's happening?"

"They're taking her straight into surgery. They think her spleen ruptured in the accident."

"Oh God." Once they got to the waiting room, Dorothy shared what she knew. "They said Mom was going across the bridge and suddenly veered off the side of the road. She'd evidently gone to the grocery store, since there were bags of food in the car. They don't know if she was trying to avoid an animal or if some kind of medical event happened. She hit a tree." She pressed a hand over her mouth. "The car is totaled and Mom…"

"She's in good hands. Dr. North has worked many trauma cases."

"She was in the army, wasn't she? Your mom talked to mine about her."

He tensed before he realized it was likely

just normal chitchat. "Yes. And like I said, she dealt with many trauma cases there on a regular basis. She knows exactly what to do."

He actually had no idea how good a surgeon Mysti was, other than what he'd seen her do for Larry. But she'd been cool and calm that whole time, so he had no reason to think this would be any different.

"Please let me get you a coffee, Dorothy. They're likely to be in there a while." He should probably call his mom and tell her about Helen, but she was watching Sally right now, and he didn't want to worry her. He'd call her as soon as this was over.

"Thank you. Just some creamer, if they have some."

"I'll be right back." Jesse got up from his seat and headed to the doctor's lounge down the hallway. Fortunately the pot of coffee in there looked fairly fresh. There was a carton of creamer in the door of the fridge.

A ruptured spleen was a medical emergency. It also meant they'd probably have to remove the organ. Helen was in her late seventies, and if she pulled through the surgery her recovery would be a long and painful one. Especially with her thinning bones.

But the lady also had a will of steel and if anyone could beat the odds, Helen would.

He fixed himself a cup to go with Dorothy's and headed back down the hallway. Handing her her coffee, he sat next to her again, listening as Dorothy shared stories of her mom and her childhood. Jesse knew that talking was sometimes the best thing to do during the long wait to hear news. He laughed when Dorothy shared some of the antics that she and his mother had gotten into when they were teenagers together.

"We were awful." Then she sobered. "I was sorry for what she went through."

He didn't have to ask to know she was talking about his father. After years of fooling around on his mother, he'd finally walked out on her, deciding to move in with his secretary, the ultimate cliché. They'd left town a month later, leaving his mom and teenage sons to pick up the pieces. None of them had spoken to him in many years. Nor had his father tried to contact him or his brother. Whether from shame or because he just didn't care, Jesse had no idea. And he had no intention of trying to find out.

"My mom had a lot of good friends to help her through things. Thank you for all you did for us."

He remembered the outpouring of love and support from people in the town. The entire community had rallied around them. It was one of the many things that kept him tied to Forgotten Point.

"Thanks for all you've done for my mom," Dorothy responded.

"She's a trouper."

"Yes, she is. I'm hoping that holds her in good stead. I'm not quite ready to…" Tears welled up in her eyes.

"I know. Let's just see where things stand when Mysti finishes with her," Jesse said gently.

Too late, he realized he'd used her first name instead of calling her Dr. North. But if Dorothy found it odd, she said nothing. Probably because they all knew one another from way back.

An hour later, Mysti came toward them. Dorothy popped out of her chair, a hopeful look in her eyes. "How is she?"

"Hanging in there. I had to remove her spleen, but there doesn't appear to be any head trauma, and there are no other areas of internal bleeding."

"Thank God."

"She's not out of the woods yet. She lost quite a bit of blood, but we're replacing that. She was stable enough after surgery that Dr. Burroughs is already in there setting the breaks in her legs. The tibia can just be casted, since the bones didn't actually separate."

"When can I see her?"

"Once Dr. Burroughs works his magic, we'll get her into a recovery room. You should be able to go in to see her then. She'll be in ICU for a couple of days just to have some additional care."

"Okay. Thank you so much," Dorothy said fervently.

"You're very welcome."

Jesse watched as Mysti drew her left shoulder in a bit as if relieving some kind of tension. Almost as if she were sore. Maybe from lifting Brutus a couple of days ago?

He decided he needed to call his mom, so she didn't hear about Helen's injuries from someone else. She was incredibly fond of Helen. He asked permission from Dorothy and then asked her, "Will you be okay here for a few minutes?"

"Yes. I need to call my daughters, anyway."

Jesse headed toward the hallway, motioning Mysti to follow him until they were out of earshot. "Are you all right? I noticed you rolling your shoulder."

Her eyes widened for a second before glancing away. "I'm fine. I was just releasing tension from the surgery. It was a close call."

The answer was quick. Too quick, as if she'd had it ready as soon as he asked. But he couldn't very well challenge her without looking like a jerk. Besides, he remembered her talking about keeping their relationship on a professional footing. "Thank you for taking such good care of her."

"Of course. I remember Helen from my childhood. She was always great with all of us. And she gave out the best Halloween candy."

"Yes, she did." Remembering Mysti as a kid in various Halloween costumes made him smile. "I may have passed by her house more than once each year."

"You wouldn't have."

He laughed at the feigned outrage in her voice. "I did. Back then I tended to help myself to whatever I wanted."

As soon as the words were out of his mouth, regret speared through his gut. Candy wasn't the only thing he'd helped himself to in his lifetime. He'd once helped himself to the woman standing right in front of him.

"Well, it's a good thing you've grown up since then."

Had he? He looked intently at her face to see if there was any hidden meaning behind her words, if she'd thought the same as he had when he'd talked about helping himself to things. But if she did, she hid it well. There was nothing there except wry amusement.

"Yes, it is." He'd grown up enough to know that you didn't snatch at things that weren't yours. At least he damned well hoped he'd learned that lesson, even if his father never had.

"Can you call me if you hear anything more about Helen?"

"I will. I promise."

"Thanks, Mysti. I appreciate it."

"You're welcome. I'd better head back and see if they need me in the OR for anything else." She gave him a wave and off she went, back the way she'd come. Leaving Jesse standing there staring after her. And sure enough, she rolled that left shoulder a couple of times as she moved away from him.

Just relieving tension, like she'd said? Or was there something else going on?

If there was, it was obviously something she didn't want or need to share with him. And he had no right to push her for answers. Because unlike when he was a kid, he wasn't going to help himself to anything that didn't belong to him—including information.

Mysti met Anna for dinner a few days later. They caught each other up on what had happened in their lives. But whereas Anna shared freely, Mysti held back. There was no reason to tell her about what had happened in Joronha or the aftermath of it.

"I'm glad you came with Jesse to collect Sally the other day. Although I'm sure I would have heard from someone that you'd come home."

"In this town? Nah." She drew the word out in a way that held unmistakable subtext.

Anna scrunched her nose. "News does tend to make its way around Forgotten Point pretty quickly, doesn't it?"

"It does. If you don't want it shared, then you'd better keep it to yourself."

"Truer words were never spoken."

Mysti smiled, taking a spoonful of her soup and swallowing. It was one of the reasons she hadn't spoken about her injury to anyone. Even when she'd been rushed back to the medical tent, she'd refused to let them call her mother to let her know what had happened. She hadn't wanted anyone to know. She still didn't. So she still hadn't told her mom. The scars on her back were hers alone to bear. And they were nothing compared to dying, like Laura had.

When Jesse had noticed her using her shoulder to stretch the still-tight scar tissue back there, it had shocked her. The move, left over from her physical therapy days, had become such a habit that she didn't even notice herself doing it anymore. And no one else had ever questioned the reflexive act. Not even her mom.

So why had Jesse asked her about it?

She had no idea. But she wasn't going to assign any special meaning to his question. He was a geriatrics doctor and probably dealt with arthritis in his patients all the time. So maybe it was something he subconsciously looked for.

Yes, that was probably it. And although she didn't have problems with the joint at this point in her life, she could imagine she might. Someday.

Anyway, he seemed to have bought her

explanation. And it was time she forgot about Jesse and focused on the conversation!

"So you're married now," she asked her old friend.

Anna nodded. "I am. And I have two boys. Would it be weird for me to take my phone out and show you pictures?"

"No, of course not."

It wasn't, but Mysti couldn't prevent a pang from going through her when she saw the smiling faces of Anna's husband and sons. "How old are the boys?"

"Seven and ten."

The younger one was the same age as Jess's daughter. The pang deepened.

Sally had probably brought Kandid so much joy. If she'd been Mysti's child, she would have...

But she wasn't Mysti's. She firmly pushed any other thoughts away.

Probably a lot of her high school friends had children in about that age range.

Even Laura had been well on her way to—

Think about something else.

"I don't recognize your husband. Is he from here? Although it's been fifteen years, so maybe he's changed."

With light sandy hair and a tall, athletic

build, she could see what had attracted Anna to him.

"Nope, I met him in college, actually. University of Kentucky."

"And you came back to live in Forgotten Point?"

She grinned. "This town doesn't like to let go of anyone. And my husband loves it here. He grew up in the city. I kept expecting the small-town charm to wear off eventually, but so far, it hasn't. He's an architect, so he does a lot of his work from home, even though he has an office in Louisville. So he has an hour-and-a-half commute on days that he meets with clients."

"And he doesn't want to move closer to his office?"

"He says no. And I'm just as glad. Having my boys grow up in a house down the street from where I grew up is something I can't get anywhere else."

"No. It's not." Mysti hadn't regretted not having children earlier in her life, but now she couldn't seem to get away from constant reminders that she was thirty-three and there were no prospects for romance. No prospects of a baby daddy of any kind, actually. Not that she wanted to go the route of having a child with someone who wasn't part of her life.

But there were plenty of women who used sperm donors and went it on their own. Why hadn't she?

Maybe because too many soldiers had died on her operating table leaving loved ones—wives and children, brothers and sisters—behind. Could she in good conscience ask her mom to raise a child if something happened to her? Even if she chose the adoption route, it could happen. She felt like she had been away from Forgotten Point long enough that there was no friend close enough to ask to take on that responsibility. Maybe in a few years she'd settle down someplace. But not right now. And once she turned forty…

She shook her head, getting irritated with herself. It did no good to sit here and long for something she couldn't have!

"I used to think you and Jesse would make a cute couple," Anna commented.

Oh, no. No, no, no.

This was not a path she wanted to wander down. "Really? But Jesse only had eyes for Kandid. After all, he married her."

"Yes, he did. But without wandering into gossip, I don't think they had the happiest marriage. The summer before they tied the knot, he looked almost… I don't know. Sad."

Mysti hadn't even stopped to wonder if Jesse's marriage had been solid. She'd always assumed it had been, that whatever had transpired between them in his car that night had been a tiny blip on his radar. He'd talked about being like his dad. Maybe that's why he'd been sad. She'd tried to reassure Jesse that night that he was nothing like him, but maybe she should have tried harder.

"I wasn't here, so I wouldn't know about that. He definitely loves his daughter, though."

"Yes, he does." Anna lifted her wineglass. "Anyway, none of that matters. I'm just happy you're home."

Mysti forced a smile and nodded in agreement. "I am, too. Even if it's just for three months."

"Really? Are you leaving again?"

"Maybe. I haven't really let myself think beyond my temporary contract at the hospital."

Especially since she was already wondering if she'd done the right thing in coming back. If she'd thought she could come here and wipe away the ghosts that had followed her back to Washington from Joronha, she'd been wrong. They'd trailed along behind her, making the twinges in her back and shoulder more pronounced. Worse, in Forgotten Point, there were other kinds of ghosts to contend with, too. Memories of her dad, whom she hadn't gotten the chance to say goodbye to. And the memory of a certain kiss that she had never received closure on.

But right now, she was here. And all she could do was try to make the best of it. Until it was time for her to pack up and move. Again.

CHAPTER FIVE

SUMMER ARRIVED IN a blaze of heat that wilted plants and people alike. Larry was coming back in for a checkup in about a half hour, and he'd wanted to kill two birds with one stone and have both Mysti and Jesse examine him together to give him the all clear to participate in the fishing tournament the following week. It was just as well, Jesse figured. This way he and Mysti could get some logistical things worked out for the tournament, such as a meeting place and time.

And it seemed like a better plan than meeting with her alone. Because when he did, his thoughts overreached into other areas. Areas she herself had forbidden them to go.

So he texted Mysti to see if she was still going to be able to be there when Larry came to his office.

A few minutes later, his phone pinged.

Meet you at your office in a few.

The text was short and to the point. But then again, his had been, too. And his idea had been to meet at the exam room first, not at his office. So much for not being alone with her.

He cleared his desk off, not because he was afraid someone would look through his paperwork, but because he didn't want it to look cluttered.

For Mysti?

Better not to answer that one.

A few minutes later, someone knocked on his door. "Come in."

Mysti poked her head around the corner. "I wasn't sure if you had another patient before Mr. Rogers."

"Nope, come on in. He's my next patient. He should be here any minute."

She slid into the room and sat in one of the chairs parked in front of his desk. She crossed her long legs, one slender limb swinging back and forth. He pulled his glance back up to her face just as she spoke. "Mom said Helen is doing okay?"

"Yes. I'm sure you've heard that she was

released from the hospital yesterday and is in a skilled nursing facility. I'm supposed to go check on her tomorrow. But her prognosis is looking far better than it could have. Thanks to you."

"There were a lot of folks involved in her care, including you. Did they find out what happened?" She slid clasped hands over her knee.

"According to her daughter, a dog darted in front of her, and Helen swerved to miss it and couldn't regain control."

"It's kind of what I'd thought. She looked very capable of driving, despite her age."

A nurse stuck her head in the room. "Mr. Rogers is here in exam room two. Are you ready for him?"

"Yep. We're on our way."

They got up from their chairs, and he motioned for Mysti to precede him through the door.

When they arrived, Mr. Rogers was already sitting in one of the chairs.

"How are you feeling?" Mysti asked.

"Like a new man."

"No more belly pains?"

"None other than the scars from the incisions pulling every once in a while."

Mysti's shoulder moved in what looked

like a half shrug. But it wasn't. It was the same movement she'd done on other occasions. Did she have a scar back there? From shoulder surgery, maybe? What had she called it the last time he'd asked? Oh, yes, shoulder tension caused by leaning over an operating table. But as far as he knew, she hadn't done surgery at all today.

"That's understandable," she said. "Do you mind if we examine you?"

"You make me sound a fish you're getting ready to gut."

Mysti gave a choked sound that she covered with a cough.

Jesse grinned. "Wrong venue, Larry. I think your mind is already on the tournament."

"Just planning my victory speech."

"I bet Mysti will give you a run for your money." He motioned to her to go ahead and start the exam.

"This is your medical practice," she said. "Why don't you do the honors?"

"But you're his surgeon," he insisted with a smile.

Larry's eyes swung from one to the other. "Hell, you sound like an old married couple. I hope you don't plan to do that during the tournament or you'll scare all the fish away."

Mysti's shoulder twitched.

Damn it, this was ridiculous. "Why don't you hop up on the table, Larry?" Jesse suggested.

Larry used the steps beside the bed to climb up. "I take it I'll need to undo my trousers. Good thing I wore clean shorts."

This time Mysti made no move to cover her laugh. God. He'd loved that laugh when they were younger. It was one of the things that had knocked down his defenses in the car when they'd been thwarted from crossing into town by water crashing over the bridge. Low and throaty, there was something sexy and seductive in the sound. It made you want to know all her secrets, want to know what it might be like to...

"I do need to look at your belly, Mr. Rogers."

Her words brought him back to reality with a bump.

"Please call me Larry. Everyone else in this town does."

Larry undid his shirt and the front of his slacks. Mysti moved closer at the same time Jesse did, and they almost collided.

That delectable laugh came again. "You first."

Gritting his teeth, he pulled out his stethoscope and used it to check the man's heart and lungs, carefully listening for any signs of congestion. It was all clear. He quickly checked his throat and eyes and ears.

"All this for my belly?" Larry's voice carried a hint of irritation, but it was made up. He had a reputation for being irascible, but it was all just a cover. Inside the man was a marshmallow.

"It's hard enough to get you into my office. I have to do it while I've got you here. Good thing you had that bellyache."

Larry made a disgusted sound. "Next time you have a part of your intestines squeezed by a...a...what was it called?"

"An adhesion." Mysti's voice was full of amusement.

"That's it." He looked up at Jesse. "If you get an adhesion, don't expect a shred of sympathy from me."

"Yes, sir." Jesse took a couple of steps back, giving her a mock bow. "He is all yours."

She moved forward, pulling out her own stethoscope as she listened to his abdomen. "Some good sounds coming out of there, Larry. You said it's still tender?"

"A little. More if I move the wrong way."

She coiled her stethoscope and slid it back in her pocket before using her fingertips to press on his belly around where the incisions were. At one point he winced. "Is it worse here?" she wanted to know.

"Yes."

"That's where I had to strip away the adhesion. There was probably some bruising. How are your bowel movements, back to normal?"

"I'm still taking that stool softener, but things are moving through, and I'm back to being hungry."

"Very good." She took a step back and held out her hand to help him up.

Uh-oh. That was a mistake. Jesse had been called out on more than one occasion for trying to aid the man. With anything.

Larry didn't snap at her, however, he simply ignored her hand and sat up on his own. Wow. He guessed there was a first time for everything.

"I'd say you're well on your way to being back to normal. You can ease off on the stool softeners unless you're starting to strain when you use the bathroom. But let me or Jesse know if that happens."

She'd used his first name and hadn't caught it. But evidently neither had Larry, since he simply nodded. "So I'm cleared to go to the tournament?"

"I would say so. May the best fisherman win."

"That's all I wanted to hear. I'm still expecting you to be there, though."

"I will be. I don't have a boat, so Jesse... er, Dr. Grove has offered to let me be a passenger on his."

That time she'd caught it. But he kind of liked that she'd let his name slip out. It made something warm settle in his gut, sending out long tendrils that reached other parts of his body. He could remember another time she'd said his name, her husky whisper making him want to take things much, much further than they'd actually gone.

"You taking that girl of yours out there, too?"

"Yes, Sally is looking forward to it."

Larry got a speculative gleam in his eye that Jesse didn't like. Maybe talking Mysti into going with him had been a mistake. He certainly didn't want the town to start talking about the two of them, or for Sally to get an idea that wasn't true. An idea that would end up hurting her.

But he couldn't very well blurt out to Larry that they were just friends. For one thing, he wasn't sure that they were. For another, it would look like a denial of something no one had even mentioned. And he didn't want Mysti to feel awkward and decide not to go to the tournament with him and Sally.

Because he wanted her there with them. He wasn't sure why. Maybe just because it had been a long time since he'd done anything fun with a woman. And Sally would be there to chaperone.

Did he need a chaperone?

If he even had to ask that question, he evidently did. And if he really thought about it, there would be a whole lake full of chaperones, wouldn't there?

Larry slid off the table. "Well, I know you're going in order to keep an eye on me, and to be honest, I appreciate it. But that doesn't mean I'm going to go easy on you. I still intend to win that tournament."

"I never had any doubt that you're going to give it all you have. You always do."

Jesse sent him out to the reception desk, but stayed in the exam room with Mysti. "So what do you really think? He'll be okay out there?"

"I think so. As long as he doesn't jump into the lake and start doing the breaststroke he should be fine."

"He'll be wearing a life jacket. We all have to."

"I know. I used to go out with my dad, remember?" She tilted her head. "You never did the tournament with your brother and dad when you were young?"

"My dad wasn't the fatherly type."

"Oh, Jess, of course. I'm so sorry."

It was something they'd talked about when they were in his car, before she confessed she was leaving and he'd kissed her. Jesse had poured his heart out to her about what his dad had done to his mother. But why should she remember? He'd been nothing to her.

"It was all a long time ago. I wouldn't expect you to remember everything I told you."

"No, I didn't mean that." She closed her eyes for a second before moving closer to touch his hand and look up into his face. "I actually remember everything we talked about that night. What I said about you doing the tournament with your dad was just something I threw out to make conversation. Because I was nervous."

About being alone with him? Hell, that was somehow even worse.

"If you're worried about me trying something with you, then don't. Like I said that was all a long time ago."

Her left shoulder slid forward then back. "I'm not worried about you…"

His eyes narrowed as they looked down into hers. If she wasn't worried about him making a move on her, then what?

I'm not worried about you.

So she was worried about herself?

Her fingers were warm on his hand, where they still touched him. Her face was still tilted up toward his, like a beautiful flower to the sunshine.

His hand turned over and caught hers, using it to tug her forward. His other hand slid up her back until his fingers were buried in her silky hair. He stared at her for a long time, his innards warring with his brain. "So, according to Larry, we sound like an old married couple, do we?"

"Evidently."

His head moved closer until his mouth hovered over her tempting lips.

But you're not married.

And he'd been down this road once before, almost to his ruin. He'd found out the hard way he wasn't exactly marriage material, hadn't he?

His teeth clenched so hard a sharp twinge went through his jaw, running up until it hit his temple.

He pulled back, swallowing down a wash of bile. Mysti's eyes opened and she frowned before realization dawned. She jerked back, blinking hard, a tide of color rushing up her cheeks.

"Hell, Myst. I'm sorry. So sorry."

She held up her hand to stop him. "Don't. This…this can't happen again. It was my fault this time, I know, but it still can't."

"I agree," he said stiffly.

She sucked down an audible breath, her teeth coming down on her lower lip. "I need to go. Thanks for letting me come examine Larry."

With that, she turned and opened the door, letting it close behind her. He didn't attempt to follow her. Even if he wanted to with every fiber of his being, what was he going to do? Catch her wrist and whirl her around in the waiting area of his office? In the busy hallway outside of it?

Besides, what more was there to say? She'd already said everything his brain had been chanting at him: this can't happen again.

She was right. It couldn't. And he was

going to see to it that there was never an opportunity for it to. No matter how hard that might prove to be.

He'd wanted to kiss her. She'd seen it in Jesse's eyes. In the way his face, his mouth had been so close to hers. And the burn in her chest when he'd pulled away… It had hurt.

This time it hadn't taken a police officer to haul them apart. All it had taken was Jesse's good sense to kick in. He'd been stronger than her last time.

And he'd been stronger this time, too.

Hell, he had chosen Kandid over her, so why wouldn't he be?

What was it about him that she couldn't resist? An ages-old crush? The memory of their last kiss? She had no idea, other than the fact that he'd been her first real honest-to-goodness kiss. And the fact that no one else had ever measured up to it afterward. She would have said she'd built the event up in her mind to proportions that no one would be able to live up to, except she'd felt that exact same heady ache as he'd come closer to her just now. As he'd murmured about them being an old married couple.

In that moment, she'd desperately wanted

that to be true. Wanted to be the old married couple Larry had called them.

Was the long-ago crush not dead after all, then? Even after all this time?

If not, then it was just a phantom ache, a remembered need that had faded away a long time ago, like those soldiers who lost limbs but then still continued to feel them years later.

So what was she going to do about it?

She could back out of the tournament, but then Larry would ask questions and might just get a little too close to the truth. And Jesse might also guess just how much he'd affected her. Because she hadn't been the one to pull away. He had. And that was the hardest pill of all to swallow.

No, she'd go on that tournament, and pretend to have a freaking fantastic time—although she'd never been that great an actor. If she could focus all her time and attention on Sally instead, maybe she could get through it. She'd concentrate on helping Jesse's daughter while he drove the boat or whatever else he needed to do. She could pack them a lunch and spend time putting everything out and then picking it back up. That should take up an hour or so.

Yes. She would just plan out her day next

week. And all of it would revolve around things that had nothing to do with Jesse and that had everything to do with surviving until her contract was up.

CHAPTER SIX

"WHAT CAN I do to help?"

Mysti's question came from the passenger seat as they waited in line at the boat launch of Lake Serenity. But Jesse noticed she didn't turn to look at him.

The huge man-made lake spanned the towns of Forgotten Point and Serenity, curving like an amoeba and forming smaller bodies of water that connected with the main part of it. Those nooks and crannies provided great hiding places for fish and made angling a very popular sport in both towns.

He made his answer matter-of-fact. He had to remember his daughter was in the back seat. So no discussing what had so nearly happened between them in the exam room. "Once we've checked in, you can help guide me into the water and hold the boat while I park."

"Okay. I did that plenty of times with

my dad." This time she gave a small smile, glancing into the back seat. "Are you excited, Sally?"

"Yes, but…" She made a face. "Do I really have to wear a life vest? I know how to swim."

Jesse opened his mouth to give a stern answer, but Mysti beat him to it. "I'm a very good swimmer, and I'm going to wear one. We all have to. If there was an Olympic swimmer out here, even he or she would have to wear one."

"Okay. As long as you're wearing one, too."

"I will. And I bet I can beat you in how fast I can put mine on."

Sally giggled, which made him frown. He wanted his daughter to be nice to her, but he hoped she didn't get attached to Mysti in some way. This was why he'd been so careful not to bring women home with him before. Not that there'd been more than a couple over the last three years. Maybe he should pull Mysti aside and talk to her about it.

After what had happened? What better way to say, "Hey, don't get the wrong idea about me leaning over you last week" than to ask her to back off from his daughter!

No. He was sure Mysti wouldn't want Sally clinging to her like a limpet, so she'd be careful. Especially since she wasn't even planning on sticking around for too long. What did she have left? Only two months of her three-month contract? She hadn't been able to get out of town fast enough after high school. And it didn't look like she was going to stay this time, either.

All the more reason for Sally not to grow to love her.

It was their turn. He registered the trio and then turned his vehicle around so the boat trailer was facing the water.

He finally glanced at the passenger seat. "Ready?"

"Can I go help Mysti?" asked Sally.

Jesse's foreboding grew a little stronger. "I need your help in the car, pumpkin. You can look out the back window and tell me how I'm doing." There was no need to tell her that the backup camera on his SUV would give him a pretty good idea of where they were.

"Okay."

Mysti jumped out of the car. In her faded blue shortalls and pink button-up shirt, she was cool and casual, a look he hadn't seen on her since high school. And those damned legs were still long and slender and more than one time he'd imagined what it might feel like to have them wrapped around…

Not happening, he told himself sternly.

She motioned him to back up, indicating when he was drifting too far to one side or the other. Right when he thought he might be getting in too deep, she held her hands up, forming a T that he took to mean stop. Putting the car in Park, he started to get out of the vehicle, but she came up to the window. "I'll crank the boat into the water. That way you won't have to leave Sally in the car by herself."

"Are you sure?"

"Yep. Like I said, I've done this with my dad hundreds of times."

Mysti had had a good father. One who'd loved her and her mom and had spent his whole life being true. That's the kind of father and husband Jesse had wanted to be. He just hadn't realized how hard it would become when you couldn't give your partner what they wanted. What they needed.

As bad as their marriage had become, he'd mourned Kandid's passing. Was glad that there was peace between them at the end. Holding her hand that last night was one of the hardest things he'd ever had to do, except for trying to explain to a four-year-old child why her mother was never coming home again.

He glanced in the backup camera to see that Mysti had already released the straps and was indeed cranking the boat down. When she switched to her left hand, he noticed she turned the winch's handle a couple of times before stopping briefly, putting her hand on her shoulder and rotating it.

It hurt. That was no "release of stress" movement. There was an actual problem with her shoulder. Why lie to him about it? Was she afraid of someone thinking she wasn't competent as a surgeon if they found out? He knew better. But why not seek out help for it? Unless it was something she already knew couldn't be fixed.

Just as he was preparing to get out of the car to help her, she'd switched back to her right hand, and the boat slid into the water with a whisper of sound. Then, holding the line at the front of the bow, she released the hook of the winch. Someone to the side stepped up and wound it back up. Then he was free to pull the trailer out of the water and go park. He had loaded all of their supplies onto the boat when they'd first arrived in the loading area, including their life vests.

He reminded himself to put Sally's on her before she actually stepped onto the boat. Then they got out of the car and made their way over to Mysti.

He hadn't seen Larry yet, but the plan was to meet at a specific section of the lake. Except he hadn't thought to ask which boat launch the other man would be using.

Mysti had already donned her vest and was in the boat, organizing some of the supplies. Although Kandid had claimed to love the water, she'd seemed fearful of being on it and concerned for Sally's safety, which was one reason they hadn't used the boat much. That and the fact that their arguments had slowly grown worse again after their daughter's birth. Kandid certainly wouldn't have volunteered to launch the boat on her own.

Hell, the last thing he needed to do was keep comparing the two women.

"Thanks," he said, noting that his and Sally's vests were already lying on the dock, ready for them. Mysti had brought a picnic hamper as well, which had been pushed in front of one of the seats so it wouldn't go flying once they got under way.

For the first time since what happened in the exam room, his mood lifted and he found he was looking forward to being out there on the water with his daughter and Mysti. He hadn't taken a real day off in ages. Oh, he'd spent his free days with Sally or with his mom and Sally, but he hadn't been on an actual outing with his child in quite some time.

After getting their vests on, he helped his daughter onto the boat, then he got in, making sure everyone was in their seats before he started the engine. Then he slowly backed away from the dock to let the next person waiting in line into the launch area.

The tournament's goal was to see who'd caught the largest fish by the end of the day.

"Everyone ready?"

Mysti smiled. "Yep, I think we are, right, Sally?"

"Ready!"

His daughter and the surgeon were seated on one of the seats that had been folded flat to form a bench. Mysti's long legs were stretched out in front of her, her hair once again pulled into a practical high ponytail. He appreciated her looking after Sally. Once they found their spot it would be easier. He'd put up the canopy to provide some shade when things got too hot. The nice thing about the bowrider was they could sit or fish from the seating area at the front of the boat. Sally had wanted to sit up there right off, but Mysti had insisted it was safer in the back until they'd reached the fishing area.

He inched up the speed, and the bow lifted a bit as they headed for a spot on the far side of the lake. Within ten minutes they'd pulled into one of the outcroppings that so far no one had claimed. The benefits of getting on the lake fairly early.

"What are we using as bait?" Mysti asked.

"I brought minnows, worms and artificial lures, so take your pick."

"Nice."

He steered into a likely spot, then threw over the anchor, making sure it was on the bottom before turning the boat's engine off.

"I haven't been on the water in so long," she murmured. "This is nice. Thanks for offering to go with me. I might have wound up in a rowboat otherwise."

He smiled. "It would have taken you a little longer to get here."

"Just a little."

As he was getting the large canopy in place, Sally went with Mysti to explore the front of the boat, where the U-shaped seats could hold several people. "Do you water-ski off this boat as well?"

"I haven't, but it's powerful enough that we could. Why? Do you ski?"

"I used to. But I haven't done it in a long time."

"We'll have to come again when there are fewer boaters on the lake." The words were out before he could stop them. Mysti's face turned toward him, a slight frown between her brows.

Of course she wouldn't want to come water-skiing with him. That whole "keeping things on professional footing" thing rearing its head again.

And those few moments in the exam room? She'd seemed pretty receptive when he'd leaned forward to kiss her.

Before he could think of a reason for offering to take her out on the water again, she said, "Actually, I think my skis are still at my mom's house."

So she wanted to come?

Warmth unfurled in his gut that he couldn't seem to get rid of. But thankfully Sally's attention was on the water over the side of the boat. She hadn't heard the invitation. Well, if he did bring Mysti back out here, he was going to leave Sally at his mom's house.

He might be stupid enough to go out on

another outing with her, but he wasn't going to involve his daughter in his foolishness. And when Mysti steadied Sally with a hand, when the little girl leaned out a bit too far, he knew he was right in worrying. The surgeon seemed wholly focused on Sally, barely throwing him a periodic glance.

She didn't have children of her own, so he'd half expected her to feel awkward having Sally with them, but she was clearly a natural with kids, shifting forward to listen carefully to something the child said and responding with a smile.

He didn't want her to be a natural with kids. Right?

Right. The last thing he needed right now was complicated.

They'd just set their hooks—Mysti had baited Sally's before he'd even finished his own—when a bass boat slid by. Larry and his son. Jesse gave a wave, knowing some fishermen liked silence while they fished. Mysti cocked her head and gave a thumbs-up sign to the man in the next boat. Larry nodded and returned the sign.

Was there anything this woman couldn't do? He was beginning to think not.

Giving a sigh, he settled into one of the white bench seats at the front of the boat with its other two occupants and prayed the day went by quickly.

So far, her plan had worked. She'd been able to concentrate mainly on Sally while keeping her gaze averted from Jesse's tanned limbs as he stood at the helm in khaki shorts and the boat shoes that provided traction on the deck. Her choice of sandals was probably a mistake, but the sun was so nice today that she couldn't resist trying to get a few rays.

And now that he was seated not fifteen feet away from where she was? Well, it was harder than it had been a few minutes ago.

She'd baited her hook with one of the minnows in the bait bucket and Sally's had a worm. Might as well see what was biting. "What'll you have?" she asked in a low voice to Jesse, whose line hadn't yet been cast.

"What do you suggest?"

The smooth way he said that made her glance his way.

Stop it, Mysti. He's talking about bait, nothing else.

"I don't know yet. Maybe try one of the artificial lures? I already have live baits on ours."

"Fake it is."

Sally was tugging at her life jacket. "It's hot."

"Do you want to go in the shade, Sally? I'll watch your hook." Her gaze swung to Jesse. "Did you bring sunscreen for her? I have some I can put on her, if not."

"I brought some." He dropped his rigged line into the water. "Mind watching that while I put some on her?"

Was there a slight emphasis on the word *I*? Okay, well, maybe fixing her attention on Sally looked like bossiness to him. Or maybe he just didn't like someone else taking care of his child. She could understand either of those options. But if she couldn't pay attention to Sally, then what could she pay attention to?

Her gaze went back to Jesse yet again.

No. She had to find something to do. Something that didn't involve staring at the hunky doctor with starstruck eyes.

She wasn't starstruck.

He was just dangerous to her self-control as he'd proved on more than one occasion.

Jesse spread a thick layer of sun protection on his daughter, working it under the straps of her life vest, then turned to her with the bottle still in his hand. "Need any?"

"No, I put some on before I left the house."

Thank God for that. Besides, she hadn't even worn a bathing suit, because there was no way she was going to prance around the boat in it. And she didn't want him to see her scars. It was also why she didn't wear sleeveless shirts or sundresses. The puckered mark covered her shoulder blade and the top of her shoulder. He'd already noticed her habit of stretching the skin using movements of her shoulder. She didn't want to give him anything else to think about.

Pulling out an electronic device, he settled Sally in a chair in the shade of the tarp before turning back to Mysti. "Feel free to come into the shade if you get too hot."

"Thanks, but the sun feels wonderful. I think I'll just stay here for a bit."

Admonishing Sally to not get out of the chair without calling to one of them, he moved to the bow to join her. "I see that you brought some lunch, too. I actually brought enough for all of us."

That made her laugh. "So did I. What did you bring?"

"Sandwiches and chips. You?"

"Fried chicken, potato salad and some watermelon. I have ice packs in there to keep everything cool."

He smiled. "I can see who's going to be the most popular one on this trip."

"We could always ask Larry and his son to join us."

They glanced over at the other boat. It looked like the two men were very serious about their fishing. Neither was talking, and they were sitting on opposite ends of their boat.

"Did your dad fish like that?" Jesse asked curiously.

"Um, no. We were probably the bane of the tournament. We were always laughing about something."

"That sounds like the opposite of being a bane."

"No. Because fishermen like quiet. Even Larry warned us about carrying on near him."

Jesse's lips pursed. "I thought he was talking along the lines of people horsing around, throwing each other into the lake, that kind of thing."

"I think that might get us a permanent banishment from the tournament. Besides, when I was a kid, I'd never heard of brain-eating amoebas back then."

"I haven't heard of a case coming out of Lake Serenity."

She gave a shrug that was only half-joking. "It's been a very warm summer, so far. So no, I don't plan on jumping into the water anytime soon."

Jesse kicked his shoes off and propped his feet up on the cushions next to her hip. A warm sensation sloshed through her at how close to her they were. His feet were only a couple of shades or so lighter than his legs, and the image of him padding around his house barefoot lodged in her brain. The warmth grew and she forced herself to look at the poles that were sitting in holders on the bow of the boat. The tips flickered with the movement of the water, but so far there were no bites.

"I can't tell you the last time I took a real day off." He glanced toward where Sally was sitting, her face bent over the electronic device she held in her hand. "I probably shouldn't let her play with that tablet, but she normally has to do homework or chores before getting screen time, so this is a break for her as well."

"Yeah, it's been a while since I've been out on a boat. When I was deployed I saw a whole lot of sand, but there was no water in sight."

"It was hard."

She didn't want to ruin his day with tales of what it was like having to be constantly on your guard, so she simply said, "Yes. It was hard."

He leaned forward. "Thank you for your service, Myst. I knew you were going to sign up, but I was surprised when your mom said you'd qualified to be a doctor, too."

"They paid for my medical degree. It seemed a small price to pay at the time."

In the end, while she hadn't paid with her life, she'd seen plenty who had. And she realized the price wasn't small at all. Not for her, and especially not for the families of those who had made the ultimate sacrifice.

"It's a price not many are willing to pay."

"Someday, I hope there's no need for anyone to. It's made me realize how valuable the job is that we as doctors do. We patch up broken people. Or at least we try. And at least we're not the people who cause them to break in the first place."

"Yes."

The word was drawn out in a way that made her wonder if he was thinking about his wife and how it had been impossible to patch her up. Sometimes all their efforts were in vain. But it didn't stop them from trying.

She sighed, glancing across the water at the other boat. "We do what we can, right?"

"And we celebrate the times when it's enough to give someone another chance. Like Larry."

Silence fell over their boat for a few minutes. With the warmth of the sun beating down on her, she found her head jerking. What the hell? She shouldn't be tired.

Well, she hadn't exactly gotten a good night's sleep last night. The thought of being out here, like a little family, had hit her hard. Because they weren't a family and never would be.

"Why don't you stretch out and take a nap?"

She shook her head. "We've only just gotten here."

"You've had a major move to contend with over the last few weeks and you've started a new job. You said it had been forever since you'd been out on the water. How about the last time you got to sleep in the sun?"

"But what about Sally?"

"She'll be fine. I've been taking care of her on my own for the last three years. And shockingly, she's still alive."

"I didn't mean that…but…"

Maybe taking a nap would be a good

thing. No need to make small talk with Jesse. No need to keep glancing over at him and imagining impossible scenarios.

No need to think. About anything.

So she nodded. "Maybe just for fifteen minutes then."

He set his feet on the ground. "Stretch out. I can change the angle of the awning to catch the shade."

"No need. I like the sun."

So Mysti did as he suggested and lay across the cushions where his legs had just been. There was a weird kind of intimacy in the act that she didn't want to explore.

And the cushions were surprisingly comfortable. "You won't steal whatever latches onto my pole, will you?"

"Isn't there a saying in the fishing world? Whoever lands it claims it?"

She giggled. "No, that is definitely not a saying."

"Okay. You'll just have to trust me, then."

"Promise you'll wake me up if you get a bite."

He stood, smiling down at her. "I don't think there'll be any sleeping through that, since the poles are behind you. Get some rest. I promise I'll wake you if anything important happens."

With that, she threw her arm over her face and closed her eyes, letting the gentle rocking of the boat and the clean smell of the lake lull her into a sense of contentment. It might not be real. And it might only be for a little while. But for the first time in a very long time, she felt…at peace.

"Mysti, wake up!" His urgent voice penetrated the lovely fog that had come over her, and she came to with a weird sense of confusion. It took her a minute to realize she was still on Jesse's boat and his hands were shaking her shoulder. The sun was warm and lovely and she didn't really want to wake up.

"What is it?" Her eyes opened and the second she saw the look on his face she sat straight up. "Is it Sally?"

"No. But something's wrong with Larry, and I need your help with him."

CHAPTER SEVEN

SHE LEAPED TO her feet, all semblance of sleep shaken off in an instant. Turning to look at the other boat, she realized Larry was slumped in his seat, his son standing over him trying to get a response.

He could have been asleep, just like she'd been, but she knew deep down he wasn't.

Why had she given him the all clear to come out here? It must have been too soon.

Sally was seated back on the bench seat on the side of the boat and Jesse had already hauled in the anchor. "We're going over to him."

He started the boat and began slowly motoring toward the other vessel. "I don't want to swamp them."

"I'll call it in."

Dialing 911, she waited for an operator to come on the line, then quickly relayed what was happening.

"Stay with Sally," he called.

He'd tossed the line to Larry's son and asked him to secure it to his boat. The man quickly did, then Jesse leaped into the vessel carrying his doctor's bag. Thank God he'd thought to bring it, because she sure hadn't brought hers. What kind of army medic left without taking a medical kit?

The kind that had retired from the military. She needed to assemble a new one once she got home. But right now, she was grateful that Jesse was here, ready to take on whatever was happening with Larry.

Between Jesse and Larry's son, they managed to get the older man stretched out on the bottom of the boat, where Jesse performed a quick examination. He checked the man's pulse, then peeled apart one of his eyes, gazing into it. "Reactive," he yelled.

Mysti relayed the message back to the dispatcher on the line.

Then he pulled out his stethoscope and listened to the man's heart. When his head came up, she saw it in his face. "I need to get him to shore. Right now. Can you manage my boat?"

"Go. I'll get everything in and follow you. An ambulance is en route to the place where we launched." She glanced back to see that

Sally was slumped in her chair asleep, just like she'd been.

"Are you sure?"

"Yes. Just go!"

He looked at Larry's son and nodded. Without any further word, the man started the outboard motor and took off toward shore.

It wasn't Larry's recent surgery; it had to be a heart attack or a stroke. There'd been something in Jesse's face when he'd looked up at her.

Reeling in the lines as quickly as she could, she discarded the bait into the water. Then laying everything on the floor of the boat, she stuffed her feet back into her sandals, then woke Sally up, strapping her into the seat and telling her to hold on. "Where's my dad?"

"He's helping the people who were in the next boat."

"Are they sick?"

"One of them is. Your dad is helping them get to shore. We're going to meet them there." She looked at the girl. "Ready?"

"Yes."

Mysti started the boat, grateful that he'd left the key in the ignition. Then she turned the wheel and pushed up the throttle and headed back to shore.

Jesse was dimly aware of another boat approaching the shore. It had to be Mysti and Sally. But still he kept working, giving chest compressions on the dock, where Larry Rogers's heart had faltered and then stopped beating.

In the background he heard an approaching siren, even as Mysti helped Sally out of the boat, keeping the child halfway behind her to shield his daughter's view of what was happening. "Can I help?"

"Ambulance is almost here. Just take her somewhere else, please."

He hadn't stopped CPR, and Mysti could only thank God that they'd kept their word and were out on the lake beside the other boat.

Even that isn't always enough.

The words whispered through her head. How many times had people died despite the large number of medical personnel who were working in the tents? Plenty. So proximity didn't always equal life.

But it did equal hope. Because he was at least getting expert attention and a chance. Even if it wasn't a large one.

Why now? His heart had checked out great before surgery. But then again, Mysti had known patients who passed their treadmill stress test and then died weeks later of massive heart attacks or strokes. Problems didn't always show up ahead of time.

Like IEDs?

Or almost-kisses that blindsided you?

Or the sudden desire to have a child of your own?

Was that last one because of Sally's recent comments that she was glad her dad finally had a "girl" friend? God, she hoped not. Because she would be here for two more months and that was it. There was not much chance that she would become Jesse's real girlfriend in that period of time. Or any other amount of time, for that matter. His almost-kiss had shown her that.

Sally's fingers gripped her hand with a strength Mysti didn't expect. She'd left the boat tied to the dock next to the one where Larry's was. There was still one more open dock, just in case other people needed to come in.

"Let's go see if they have something to drink at the check-in desk."

Sally glanced up. "Is that man going to be okay?"

She wondered how much this child had seen, having a doctor as a father. "I hope so, sweetheart."

An ambulance pulled into the entrance to the lake and someone waved them over to the scene going on behind her. She made it to the folding table. "Do you have anything she could drink?"

"We have some water and juice." The woman was sympathetic. She bet everyone already knew what had happened and to whom. It was the way both of these little towns worked.

"Do you have orange juice?" Sally's voice came from beside her.

"We have apple juice, will that work?"

The child nodded. "Thank you."

"Anything for you?" the woman asked Mysti.

"Actually, I'll have the same, please."

"Coming right up."

Two bottles were produced, the ice still clinging to their sides.

Mysti thanked the woman and then made her way over to a small bench, careful to keep their backs to whatever was happening behind them. She opened Sally's bottle and handed it to her before twisting the top on her own drink and tipping it up to her mouth, drinking thirstily.

She couldn't believe she'd actually fallen asleep on his boat. But then again, she'd been exhausted. She didn't even remember much about what had transpired before that point, although she did remember the warmth of the sun on her face and laughing about Jesse's threat to steal any fish she hooked on her line.

The apple juice was cold going down, the welcome splash in her belly helping to cool her down. "Good?" she asked Sally.

"Yes. I like apple juice, too."

"So do I."

She chanced a glance behind her and saw them loading Larry into the back of the EMS unit. Jesse was nowhere to be seen. She wasn't sure if he was riding in the back of the rig or if he had just handed Larry over to the EMTs. It wouldn't matter, except she'd just realized she didn't have keys to his car. Maybe it was on the key ring with his boat keys.

But none of that was important right now. She had no idea what was going on with Larry, but at the moment, all she could do was pray and hope for the best.

*   *   *

Jesse saw them sitting at the bench over by the information desk. They were facing away from him. He watched as Mysti leaned over to say something to his daughter, his chest contracting.

The scene was a little too familiar. Like something out of the not-so-long-ago past that hadn't quite blurred completely away.

It had to be what he'd just gone through. The paramedics had managed to get Larry's heart started again, but as their eyes had met, they'd confirmed his sense that the situation wasn't good. He wasn't even sure the older man was going to survive at this point. And that look in Larry's son's eyes…

Devastation.

What he'd felt when Kandid had died, even though he hadn't loved her anymore, if indeed he ever truly had.

What he'd felt when Mysti had said she was leaving Forgotten Point to join the army, and never coming back.

As if sensing someone was behind her, the woman in question turned slightly, eyes widening when she saw him. "How is he?"

"He's hanging on, but…"

What could he say? He couldn't very well say the man probably wasn't going to make it in front of his young daughter. Right now she deserved to have a world that was happy and carefree. Sally had been too young to fully understand what had happened to her mother, but that wouldn't always be the case. A time was coming all too soon when she would realize things were not always beautiful. That people left and never came back, whether it was from dying or by virtue of moving away.

Except Mysti had come back. But only for a while.

Jesse wasn't sure right now how he really felt about that. It had been so much easier when he couldn't see her right in front of him, when there was no hope of her return.

And now that there was?

Well, she was a reminder of what he'd almost done in behaving exactly like his father. That night had shaken his world. He never wanted to feel that unsure of himself ever again.

Jesse was realistic enough to know that Mysti had the power to make him feel exactly like that all over again. Just by her presence.

Except there was no longer the possibility of cheating on Kandid, because she was no longer alive. And if Mysti had been here when he and his wife had been going through their marital problems? Would he have turned to Mysti for comfort?

God, he hoped he would have done the right thing. The honorable thing.

But there was no way of knowing for sure. Because Mysti had not been in town during that time. And even without her presence he had failed Kandid as a husband.

"Daddy, Mysti bought me apple juice."

"I can see that." He looked at the surgeon and mouthed *thank you*.

She nodded in response. "I left your boat tied to the dock. I wasn't sure what else to do with it."

"Yeah, sorry for leaving you with all of that. I didn't want to try to transfer Larry over to our boat in the condition he was in."

"Of course. You did what had to be done. And Sally and I were fine. We still had the picnic baskets on the boat if we got stranded for a bit."

"Do you want to go back out onto the water? Or are we done for the day?"

"I think we're done, if that's okay. I'd be too worried about Larry to enjoy myself." She twisted her lips to the side. "Besides, I already dumped the bait. I didn't figure we would be going back out."

"I guess that's that. Good call, though, on the bait."

He glanced at his daughter. "You want to go with me to get the truck so we can load the boat?"

"I want to stay with Mysti."

He frowned, but said, "Do you want to sit here for a while or go over to the dock?"

"I'll go over with you. I'll help winch the boat back onto the trailer," Mysti offered.

He took a step closer and touched her hand. "Thanks for your help today."

"I didn't actually help. Unless you call snoring in the front of the boat 'help.'"

He couldn't contain a quick laugh. "I wasn't going to say anything but…"

She nudged him with her elbow. "Very funny. I need to go check on Larry. After doing his surgery and thinking he was going to be okay… Then this. Can you drop me off at the hospital on your way?"

"We can both go. Let me put in a quick call to my mom and ask her to watch Sally."

"You don't have to. He's my patient."

"No, Myst. He's *our* patient. And he's a friend."

She nodded. "You're right. He belongs to both of us."

The way she said that made a spark flare

to life in his gut. He could imagine her saying that about a child. Their child. Watching her with Sally had been…

He squared his jaw. But they weren't talking about a baby or a child or anything else. It meant nothing. Mysti had walked away once before. From him. From the town. And she was poised to do it all over again. Just like his father had. It all seemed tied up together somehow, the strings all wrapped and tangled into a jumbled mess. And he'd be damned if he could sort it all out. Not now. Maybe not ever.

They pulled the boat out of the water, and he called his mom.

"Of course I'll watch my little darling. Why don't you let her stay the night again?"

His mom was too good to him. "Because I don't want to take advantage of you. She just spent the night not long ago."

"If getting to play with my only grandchild is being taken advantage of, then you should do it more often. You know she's going to want to stay over. Is that really a battle you want to fight?"

"No. It's not. Okay, thank you. Do you still have some of her things there?"

"Pajamas? Check. Clothes for the morning? Check. I'll just keep her clothes from today and wash them for next time she stays with me."

With that settled, they made a quick trip to unhook the trailer at his house. He could move it back to storage tomorrow. And then he got to his mom's house only to find Sally was asleep in the back seat. While Mysti got the door, he carefully lifted her out of the car and walked up toward his mom's old farmhouse. She was already at the front door, waiting for him.

"Oh, poor sweet darling. Bring her through here to the couch. She can take a little nap."

He hesitated. He loved his daughter so much, and leaving her anywhere was always so hard. Maybe it was because of Larry and Kandid, but the realization that life was so fragile was never far from his mind. It probably made him more protective of his child than he needed to be. Even leaving her with Mysti on that boat had taken every ounce of his willpower.

There was no way he was going to let anything—or anyone—hurt her. It was why he'd never contacted his dad. Why his father had never met his grandchild.

And being around Mysti? A person who had had no problems walking away from the town and her life here before? Well, today they'd been together out of necessity. But letting her into his daughter's life on a regular basis would be a major risk, even if they just stayed friends and never dated. He wasn't sure he was willing to chance it, no matter how much Sally enjoyed her company.

"I can always pick her up when I'm done at the hospital, Mom."

"No, let her stay." Her eyes when she looked up said so much. "Please."

"Okay."

She smiled and turned her attention to Mysti. "It's so good to see you again, Mysti. Jesse said you've only been back a few weeks."

"Yes, I…er…was discharged from the military and so I decided to take a little time to come home and get my bearings."

"I hope you're back for good."

Mysti bit her lip. "My contract at the hospital is only for three months. I haven't really thought yet about what happens after that. I wanted to see how everything felt. How working in a hospital felt."

She was only saying what Jesse already knew. She hadn't come home with the intention of staying. Had just come home to see how she did in a small hospital before moving on to something bigger and better. And with her skills those opportunities would be a dime a dozen.

After today, he was going to be extremely careful about letting Sally anywhere near her.

And himself?

Well, using her words, he was going to "see how everything felt." He wasn't a child. He was able to hold himself apart emotionally without letting anyone get too close. Hadn't Kandid always called him an expert at that?

His mom replied, "Well, we hope you'll decide stay here in Forgotten Point, don't we, Jesse?"

Hell, it was like the universe had read his mind. "I think that's Mysti's decision to make, Mom."

"Well, of course it is. But I can hope, can't I?"

Mysti took her hand. "Thank you for that. It's been good being home and seeing people I once knew."

"People you still know, dear. Time doesn't change that."

But it did. He could see it in Mysti's eyes, in the way her shoulder inched forward. Time changed a lot, and they both knew it. She wasn't the shy girl he'd once known. She and Kandid had been opposites, with her friend taking the lead in most things. Maybe it's what had drawn him to Mysti that night. She had a way of listening—really listening—that had gotten to him. He'd shared more about his father with her than he had with anyone else. And then finding out she was leaving town… Well, it was no wonder his emotions had gotten the best of him.

But they had both changed. Had learned their place in life. And that place wasn't with each other.

"Well, we need to go, Mom. We have a patient to see."

As if Mysti had suddenly realized where she was, she let go of his mother's hand and took a step back. She glanced at him. "No word on Larry yet?"

"No, I checked for texts, but so far nothing."

Saying their goodbyes, they headed out the door and got back into the car. "Sorry about my mom. She doesn't always have the best filter."

"It's fine. It's nice to know I'm wanted." Her words were soft. Pensive. And there was something behind them that made him swallow. "It was hard that last year of high school, and things didn't always… Never mind."

Had she not felt wanted back then? Hell, he hoped he hadn't added to any stress. But he couldn't change what had happened in the past—he could only affect the present. "Well, you're wanted now. I hope you know that."

"Thank you." She turned to look out the window. "I hope he's okay."

"I hope so, too."

Ten minutes later they were back over the bridge and pulling into the parking lot of the hospital. They both got out of the car, and he and Mysti hurried toward the main entrance. "He'll probably be in the cardiac unit."

"Let's stop at the main desk and check to be sure."

She glanced at the waiting room. "I don't see his son."

Could he have been transported to one of the bigger hospitals? Serenity Regional was equipped for most things—it even had a trauma center—but there were times when more specialized care was called for.

Jesse asked at the desk. "Larry Rogers was brought in here about an hour ago. I'm his primary care physician."

"The heart attack victim from the fishing tournament?" She didn't even check her screen. A flicker of warning went through him.

"Yes."

She shook her head. "I'm very sorry. He didn't make it out of the ER."

They were too late. He'd had a bad feeling about it even as he worked on Larry at the boat launch. "Is his son still here?"

"No. He was pretty distraught. Said he had family to notify."

Larry's wife had died ten years ago, and his son—their only child—had never married. There were no grandchildren. No one to share his grief with except for extended family.

"He'd seemed fine at his checkup appointment last week." Mysti's voice came from beside him. She looked…stricken.

"Yes, he did. But we can't always predict when someone will throw a clot. Or stroke out. All we can do is give them the best care we can."

"It's just never enough. Never."

He didn't think she was necessarily talking about Larry.

"Let's go somewhere and get some lunch. Neither of us has eaten, and I could use a strong cup of coffee."

Mysti nodded, her hand going to her left shoulder and rubbing at it for a second. He didn't think she was even aware she was doing it. Much like she wasn't aware of when she was working it as if trying to find a more comfortable position for it.

"I'll call Larry's son later and see if there's anything I can do." His chest squeezed at the thought. He wished there'd been something more that he could have done at the scene. But being on the lake had made everything take longer. If they could have gotten him to the hospital sooner… If he could have kept doing CPR uninterrupted instead of having to get on and off boats… None of those regrets were going to bring the old man back, though.

"I wasn't even here when my dad passed away. And there wasn't time for me to come home afterward," Mysti murmured.

Hell, he hadn't gone to her dad's funeral, either. In fact, he'd kind of avoided Mysti's mom since Mysti left. So had Kandid, come to think of it, and she'd been one of Mysti's closest friends back in school.

"That couldn't have been easy for you."

"No. None of it was easy."

Again there seemed to be more behind the words than simple grief. His chest squeezed.

"Come on, let's go into Serenity and find a place to eat."

"Okay." She looked up. "You know you did everything you could for Larry, right?"

"There were delays when every second counted. Getting to him. Getting him to shore. Getting him out of the boat."

She touched his hand. "Hey, there are always delays. You can't imagine the delays I've seen. Sometimes it makes a difference. Sometimes it doesn't. But like you said, we just do the best we can. And pray that it's enough."

CHAPTER EIGHT

THEY ATE FISH and chips out of plastic baskets at a place in Serenity. Mysti didn't remember this place being here when she was
a kid; then again, the neighboring town had
changed more than Forgotten Point had.

"You okay?"

She wasn't. But what could she say? "Why
wouldn't I be?"

"Is this your first loss since being back
here?"

Was it? She'd had so many losses over the
years. Her dad. So many soldiers. Laura...
Now Larry. The list seemed to stretch end-
lessly.

And some losses didn't include death.
She'd lost Jesse as a neighbor and Kandid
as a friend. Kandid, the one person she'd
confided in about her crush on Jesse the last
year of high school. Kandid, who'd always
had her choice of guys. She could have had

anyone. And she'd chosen Jesse. Despite knowing that Mysti cared about him. That had been the worst thing about it. There'd been no apology from her friend. No explanation.

She'd made sure to invite Mysti to the wedding, although Kandid had to know there was no way in hell that she would have come. Life in California was busy. Or that would have been her excuse. The reality was she'd run as far away from Forgotten Point as she could get without falling into the ocean. And later, after she'd qualified, and once she was posted overseas, even the ocean hadn't stopped her.

She'd never heard from Kandid or Jesse again. And she'd never asked her mom for information about either of them—or anyone else, either. And as for Jesse's question just now?

She told him the truth. "Yes, it's the first loss of a patient since I've been back."

After all, Jesse had been lost to her for a long time. And even if her crush wasn't quite dead yet, he'd made his choice perfectly clear. He'd chosen Kandid. And Mysti didn't think she could bear to be a poor replacement for the love of his life. Anna must have been wrong about Jesse's marriage not being a happy one. After three years, he wasn't even dating anyone else.

"You told me I'd done all I could. So did you. You made sure his last weeks were comfortable ones. He would have died sooner if he hadn't had the surgery—would have spent each of those days in agony. The fact that he passed away doing something he loved so much isn't necessarily a bad thing. And from what Larry Jr. said, his dad simply slumped over in his seat. He hadn't complained of chest pain and had felt great that morning. Sometimes it just happens, and there's nothing anyone can do to stop it."

Like Laura's death?

But that was so very different. She hadn't simply slipped into a painless death like Larry had. She'd been blown to pieces by a bomb set by people with the express purpose of killing other people. Mysti would never understand it. She'd never had to lift her gun to shoot at anyone. Her job was to save people. Killing went against her very nature.

But there were so many people she hadn't been able to save.

"I know. And I'm glad we were there to save his son from having to second-guess himself. Medical care was only a boat away." She looked at him. "It's good that we went together."

She had thought about backing out, but if she had then there would have been no one to take Jesse's daughter and boat back to the dock while Jesse worked on Larry. And even if they had somehow managed to transfer Larry to the other boat, it would have used up even more time.

"Yes, it was. I never thanked you for getting Sally back safely and taking care of her."

"You did. You probably just don't remember it."

If only it were that easy to forget other things, too. She took out a hush puppy and popped it into her mouth, chewing it. They weren't exactly in the seafood capital of the world, but there were things she'd missed about these two small towns.

"I'll have to take you back out on the boat on a regular day to make up for today. You did me a favor, and I really appreciate it."

"There's no need to pay me back."

"What if it's not about paying you back?"

She blinked. Was he asking her out on a date?

Before she could say anything, he went on. "My mom is afraid of the water—she can't swim, and I haven't taken Sally out by myself. Mainly because of how busy life is and the amount of work it takes to get things together to go out on the lake. But also, I don't like the thought of Sally sitting in a chair while I'm navigating and unable to make sure she's safe."

"Oh." So he wanted her as a babysitter? As soon as that thought struck her, another one came on its heels. What did it matter why he'd asked her to go? She liked Sally, liked being around a child when for years she'd only associated with adults. She'd almost forgotten the joy that came with kids' laughter and questions. "Sure. I can watch her if you want."

"I'm not asking you in order to have someone to look after her. Except for what happened with Larry, I really enjoyed being out on the boat today. I actually haven't just gotten away from the house for much of anything in a few years."

Since Kandid's death. He hadn't said the words, but she heard them beneath all of the other things he'd said. Sometimes you did just have to get away from the memories, as she'd found out from leaving Forgotten Point. As she'd found out in leaving the military. It sounded like Jesse hadn't had a chance to do any of that. And if she could help him at all…

"That sounds like fun. I miss being out on the water, too."

"We could even take a pair of water skis. You said you used to ski, if I remember right. That your mom might still have yours?"

"I did. But I don't even know if I could get up now."

"Well, you'd have to be better than I'd be. It wasn't something I did as a child."

She couldn't imagine there being much of anything that Jesse Grove couldn't do.

"You could always learn."

"We'll see." He leaned back and pushed his plate away. "So you'll go?"

"Yes. I'd love to."

He pulled out his phone and flipped through a few screens. "I don't have anything next Saturday."

"That should work. Unless there's an emergency, most of my surgeries are scheduled during the week."

"Sally will be thrilled."

And Jesse. Was he thrilled?

Maybe. But if so, it wasn't because of her. It was because he'd be able to take his daughter out on the water without worry. And get a little bit of a break himself.

He glanced outside. "Looks like it's just as well that we're not still out there. It's getting dark."

"I saw that they were predicting some rain for this afternoon, but not until later. What time is the tournament on until?"

"Five. It's about fifteen minutes until then. They're supposed to announce the winner, so everyone should be back in with their catches by now. I'm sure they'll have the weigh station inside the community center if the weather turns bad."

Suddenly, she wanted to be there. Wanted to make a suggestion to the people running the tournament. "Wouldn't it be good if they named this tournament after someone who was there almost every year without fail? Who even came weeks after having major surgery?"

Jesse's head tilted. "If you're thinking what I think you are, I like it. It's always just been called the Forgotten Point Fish-Off." He glanced at her plate. "We'll have to leave now, though, if we're going to catch the committee there."

"I'm done."

After gathering their baskets and empty drink cups, they discarded them in the trash.

* * *

The rain held off as they drove over to the landing, and there were some patches of blue that made him wonder if it was going to rain at all.

Pulling into the dirt entrance, Mysti said, "Jesse, look."

He glanced over at the landing, where there were still a couple of stragglers pulling their boats out of the water. And still moored at the edge was a familiar bass boat, bobbing in the water with no sign of its owner. "Larry's boat. His son must not have come over to get it yet."

His gut shifted. He could imagine that was the last thing on Larry Jr.'s mind. Losing his father over the course of an hour had probably rocked his world. And like Mysti had said of her own father, Larry and his son had participated in this tournament for years. Many years.

"I think I'll see if I can get in touch with someone. Maybe afterward we can pull it out and take it home for them."

"It's going to be hard for his son to deal with that. It was the last time he was with his dad."

They parked and got out of the car, heading over to the fish weighing station, which was still active, despite the darkening clouds. Next to it was a large dais housing some chairs with some microphones at the front. There was a large building behind it, where he assumed everyone would retreat to if it started pouring.

A large whiteboard was propped up and a series of numbers was written on it, going up to fifty.

"I didn't realize there were that many entries. I thought maybe numbers would have dropped off over the years."

Fifty was the maximum number of boats allowed out on the lake during the tournament for safety's sake. "Does it always max out?"

She gave him a look before murmuring, "That's right, you didn't participate in it as a kid."

Well, he had gone out on a friend's boat during it one time. It was the first time he'd realized that not all families were like his, with a father who rarely came home and a mother who spent a lot of time crying. Her life had changed for the better when his father finally walked out. It had been hard. Really hard for a year or two while they got their bearings and while his mom found a better job, but they'd managed to keep the house. Their father hadn't even fought for custody rights, he'd simply dropped out of their lives, leaving town for parts unknown. And his mom hadn't sued for child support. Jesse hadn't asked at the time, because he knew nothing about divorce settlements or how things were done. But he imagined his mom hadn't wanted to face her ex ever again. They'd never talked about it since. Jesse steered clear of any mention of his father. And his mom didn't bring it up, either.

"I didn't. But I think this might be something that Sally and I could do every year."

Something shifted in her face.

"What?"

"Nothing." Her gaze traveled the group. "I think I see Earl Norman. He used to head up the tournament. I'm not sure he's still doing it. But surely he'll know who is, if not."

They walked over, and the man glanced up from his sheet of paper. "Sorry to interrupt," Mysti said. "Do you have a minute?"

"Mysti North. I remembered seeing your name on the list of entries. Glad you're back at it. We sure do miss your daddy."

"Thanks. So do I." She paused. "You know that Larry Rogers died today."

"I heard. I couldn't believe it. We used

to say that Larry was one of the founding members of the tournament."

She nodded. "I don't remember that far back, but I believe it. Any chance you can bring up an idea to whoever is on the committee?"

"What kind of idea?"

"About making this a memorial tournament in honor of someone who supported it with all his heart."

Earl's pencil stilled on the paper. "Larry?"

She nodded. "Something like the Larry Rogers Memorial Fish-Off. Maybe we could even start a fund helping less advantaged kids take part in the tournament. Ones whose families can't afford their own boats. Or ask for people to take one of those children on their boats and let them experience the tournament firsthand."

"I like that idea. Like sponsoring a kid?"

"Yes. It wouldn't change the number of boats allowed out on the lake, it would just be a chance for kids who want to be out there to have an opportunity to participate. The sponsoring entry could provide the extra bait and bring a spare rod with them. So the cost to the committee would be minimal."

Earl nodded. "Honestly, that's a great idea. We've been kicking around something similar for years. Maybe Larry's death will finally get things moving again." He glanced around. "I think the whole committee is here, so I'll flag them down and talk to them. It wouldn't be a bad idea to announce some sort of resolution today, so we can prepare for next year's tournament."

Jesse had to hand it to Mysti. He couldn't imagine the girl he'd once known coming in here and taking the bull by the horns. But the Mysti of today?

Yes. It seemed she would. He found he liked that. Really liked the confident woman she'd become. He'd thought she was cold that first day in the hospital. She wasn't. She just knew what she wanted and wasn't afraid to go after it.

"Thank you," she said.

Earl looked at Jesse. "Good to see you and your daughter out there, too, Jesse. Your first time?"

"It's the first time I've brought a boat out myself. But I actually came with a friend one year as a kid. They kind of did for me what Mysti is suggesting now. I still remember that trip out and catching my first fish."

Mysti's head cocked as she looked over at him, but she didn't say anything. Nor did she push Earl to use that information in his pitch. And Jesse appreciated that.

A lot.

Earl closed his pad and stood. "I'll round up a few people and see what they think. I'm not sure we can get it done by the end of the afternoon, but we can try."

"Thank you."

Earl headed off toward the scoreboard, which was probably where most of the other committee members were.

"That was a really good idea, Mysti. I think Larry Jr. will be grateful."

"Thank you." She glanced over at the crowd of people sitting in folding chairs that had been woven among the trees. "Can you stay for a while?"

"Yep. I'm anxious to see what size catch is going to win."

They went over to see what was going on, finding two chairs toward the back. So far entry number fifteen had the biggest fish with a ten-pound largemouth bass.

"How big was the fish you caught that day?"

Her question took him by surprise. He'd assumed she wasn't going to mention what he'd said. Or that maybe she already knew somehow.

"Four pounds. Not nearly big enough to win."

"But big enough for you to remember. We were your neighbors. We should have invited you to come with us."

"It's okay, you had no way of knowing." That day had changed so much for him. Had made him want to be better than his own father. Had made him want to be like the dad who'd taken him out in his boat and acted like it was something he did every day. And maybe he did. Or maybe the whole town had known what kind of home he grew up in. "And yes, that fish had been big enough for me to remember."

"I hope there are lots of kids in the future who have a great experience like that to look back on."

It wasn't just that day on the water that had been a wakeup call for him. Today had been, too. Seeing the exhilaration on his daughter's face when the bow of their boat had lifted had made him realize how little leisure time he actually had with her. She was already seven. In ten years she'd be graduating from high school and probably leaving for college. He wanted to give her a life like Mysti had had with memories that were cherished long after he was gone.

And he had Mysti to thank for that for making him realize it. As much as he considered that kiss all those years ago to be a mistake, maybe it could finally bring about something good.

"I don't know that I ever fully apologized to you for what I did all those years ago."

Her shocked face swung around to look at him. "Sorry?"

"For what happened in the car."

"We were both just kids, Jess. There was no need to apologize."

"I was dating Kandid. There was a need. I was just embarrassed that I behaved like that. But I am sincerely sorry. I hope that wasn't why you left Forgotten Point."

"Nope. It wasn't because of the kiss." She sighed. "And if anyone should apologize, it should be me. Kandid was my friend. It felt like such a betrayal of her at the time."

"I know what you mean. Is that why you didn't stay in touch with her? Didn't come to the wedding?"

"Maybe." She shut her eyes. "It was so long ago. And neither of us seems to be particularly scarred by the experience. You went on to have a great marriage, and you now have a beautiful daughter. So all is well."

His marriage hadn't been great at all. But maybe those cracks hadn't been as evident to everyone in town as they were to him. And why admit to Mysti now that there had been serious problems between him and Kandid? For one thing, it wouldn't change anything; it was all water under the bridge. For another, Kandid was dead. He'd never needed to make any hard decisions about divorcing her, and he certainly didn't want Sally to know how angry he and her mom had been at each other. So, no. He wasn't going to disabuse Mysti of the notion that he'd had a perfect marriage.

"Yes, all is well."

A cheer went up over the crowd and he looked up to see that entry number thirty-one had just taken the lead with a fish that was a little over ten pounds.

"So what was your biggest fish?" He asked the question without looking at her.

"I don't remember the exact weight. But it was probably around five pounds. I remember needing my dad's help to reel it in. To me it seemed massive, and I honestly didn't care that it didn't win. It was just fun being out there. Being with my dad."

"So if the committee doesn't take up the idea, what would you think of having a competing tournament instead using Larry's name and that idea of taking more kids out on the water?" He looked at her, trying to feel out her response.

"Do you think they won't vote to do it?"

"I'm hoping they will. But I'm sitting here thinking what action I should take in the event that they don't, and I'm convinced it's the right thing to do."

"I know. My mind is whirling with the possibilities. Maybe a fund could be started to buy a fishing pole for every kid who doesn't have one but wants one. Or even putting the entry fees toward something bigger, like a bass boat that we could lend to families who would like one but couldn't afford to buy or even hire one for day." There was a sparkle in her eyes that he liked.

"I'm pretty sure some boat manufacturers would like to get in on something like that."

They looked at each other and for a second or two he couldn't look away, watching as something in her gaze changed, her pupils enlarging until they seemed huge.

Another cheer pulled his attention back to the board. They watched over the course of the next half hour as the numbers slowly crept up and more and more numbers had weights beside them. His and Mysti's number was blank as were some others, one of them being Larry's boat, of course.

Then all the fish had been weighed and the winning fish, a twelve-pound large-mouth bass, was held up by the person who'd caught it. He'd won a fishing pole and fuel for his boat for a year.

Then Earl got up on the makeshift plat-form. "I'd like to call up the members of this year's tournament committee. Most of these folks have served for a long time and have put in a lot of hard work to make this event happen each and every year. The commit-tee stocks the lake with fish with the help of a nearby hatchery, releasing two fish for every one caught at the tournament."

Applause went up as people made their way onto the platform. It looked like there were about twenty people on the committee.

"We have one other item of business be-fore we finish. Some of you may not know this yet, but we lost one of our own today. A man who looked forward to the fish-off every year."

Murmurs went through the crowd, and Earl held up his hands to quiet them down. "A suggestion was made—a great one, I might add—that we dedicate the future fish-offs to his memory and that we add a component of making it possible for disadvantaged kids to participate. How would we do that? By asking every boat that enters to consider taking on an extra passenger. We would collect names of kids who want to come, and those who are willing would draw a name, making sure they have a pole, bait and tackle, and a life vest available for that person. We'll be brainstorming more ways to give back to the community in conjunction with the fish-off. The committee was unanimous in favor of the idea, but I also want to hear from you." He waited for a beat or two. "How many of you would like to see this happen? Give us a show of hands."

Jesse swore every hand in the area went up. He searched the crowd and couldn't spot one person who wasn't in agreement.

Earl nodded, throwing a smile toward him and Mysti. "We have Mysti North and Jesse Grove to thank for the suggestion. Would you two please stand?"

Oh, hell. That was not what he'd wanted. But people had turned and were motioning for them to stand up. So they did, as the crowd clapped and gave whistles. Mysti rolled her shoulder back a time or two, so he wasn't the only one uncomfortable with the attention.

He also noticed two women look at each other and then lean forward to whisper something, smiling and nodding. Great. He was pretty sure that was going to be the start of some unfounded rumors about him and Mysti. But he could deal with a few rumors if it meant that Larry would have his Memorial Day each year.

He sat down as Earl's voice came back over the microphone. "So from today on, our annual tournament will be known as the Larry Rogers Memorial Fish-Off. Thank you all for helping to make this happen."

CHAPTER NINE

"WE DID IT," Mysti said as the first big drop of rain hit her in the forehead. She couldn't believe the committee had gotten it done that quickly. She hoped Larry's son was happy with the idea. But why wouldn't he be? Maybe they should have run it by him first, but she was pretty sure that the man would agree that his dad deserved this honor.

More drops came down as people started scrambling to get their things together to head to their cars before the bottom dropped out of the sky.

"You did it, actually. But right now I think we should make our way back to the truck before we get completely soaked."

"I agree."

Too late—the drops turned torrential within a matter of seconds. Jesse grabbed her hand and took off at a run toward the parking area where his truck was buried among those of the other participants. Her foot slid on a wet rock and if Jesse hadn't had a hold of her, she would have gone down. As it was, her hand jerked out of his. He slowed his pace, wrapping an arm around her waist to make sure he didn't lose her again.

They ducked between other folks who were just as anxious to get to their vehicles, but even with the crowd, they made it less than five minutes later.

He'd evidently used his fob to unlock the doors, because he grabbed the passenger one and yanked it open.

She hesitated. "I'll get your seat wet."

"You'll get it even more wet if you don't get in. The rain is driving straight in."

So she slid onto the leather seat, which was cool against her moist skin.

A minute later, Jesse was in his own seat.

Reaching over her, he pulled open his glove box and pulled out a couple napkins, handing her a few. She used them to mop her face, hands and legs. She shoved stray strands of hair out of her eyes, very glad she'd pulled it back in a ponytail today.

Then the absurdity of the situation hit her, and she started laughing.

"What's so funny?"

She shook her head, trying to figure out

how to tell him. "Just that we were all out there on the lake today, with the possibility of falling into the water at some time, but all it took was a little rain to make everyone take off running."

He chuckled. "You're right. We were both getting spray from the boat earlier when we were moving toward our spot and no one thought anything of it."

"Nope."

"So what is it about rain that brings on such hysteria?"

She had no idea. What she did know was that sometimes it caused people to behave in ways they might not ordinarily behave.

The memory of them locked in each other's arms in a storm very much like this one came back to her.

How could she remember it so vividly? Yet she could. The feel of his lips. The heat coming off his body. The smell of skin washed by clean water.

She swallowed, jerking when the car next to them started its engine and pulled out of its space. It hadn't taken long for people to clear out. She chanced a glance at Jesse to find him with his hands gripping the wheel, staring straight ahead.

"Jess?"

When he turned to look at her, she saw it. She wasn't the only one who remembered that night so vividly.

"This is just like…"

"I know."

Mysti wasn't sure whether she reached out first or he did, but suddenly his hands were on her shoulders urging her toward him. Since her body was already in motion, she collided with his chest, laughing as he grunted at the impact.

Her laughter was soon swallowed when his mouth came down on hers, kissing her, his tongue thrusting home as if remembering how little time they'd had that night.

She was just as desperate to kiss him, too. Most of the cars had already pulled out of the parking lot, and she was pretty sure no one who was left was interested in what they were doing. They were just trying to get into their own vehicles.

Her hands found his neck, one of the spots he'd missed when he'd dried himself with the napkin, the hair at his nape cold and wet. This kiss was even better than their youthful foray, maybe because both of them were older and had lived lives that could be both happy and tragic.

This time, there was nothing tragic about

having his arms around her. It was heady. Magical. And she never wanted it to stop.

He lifted his head far too soon, and her mind screamed a protest. "Come home with me. Just for tonight," he urged hoarsely.

Go home with him?

Her brain was foggy with desire, and she didn't think she could say no, even if she wanted to. Because she didn't want to. She had dreamed about what being with him might be like long after she'd left town. And unlike last time, there was no guilt...no one standing between them.

That last phrase brought with it a whisper of caution, but she ignored it. Tuned it out.

"Yes."

He stared at her dazedly as if he couldn't believe what he was hearing. Then his head came down again, and he kissed her deeply, his mouth moving over hers as if he couldn't get enough of the taste of her. Fingers trailed down her neck, the feathery touch sending shivers over her skin as they slid over her shoulder and down her side, just grazing the edge of her breast. "We need to go. Or we won't make it out of the car. And if a police car comes up this time, we might not be found just kissing."

Her nipples puckered instantly. She wanted

him so desperately. In the car. In his house. Wherever she could get him. After all this time this need for him was still as sharp as it had been fifteen years ago. Maybe even more, since she now knew how fragile and temporary life could be.

All thoughts of the tournament were forgotten as Jesse navigated the streets in the rain, his palm resting on her upper thigh, thumb brushing over the skin just beneath her shortalls and sending a shudder through her that had nothing to do with being chilled from the rain.

Unlike all those years ago, the bridge didn't have water sluicing over it, and they crossed it with ease. There was nothing blocking the path to what they wanted. At least for tonight.

It was okay, right? Just this one time. He had clarified that for her, so she didn't have to worry about there being any hint of commitment in play here, because she didn't think she could do that. Not with him. Not knowing he'd chosen someone else over her once upon a time, to be his wife and the mother of his child. She didn't know why that mattered, and she didn't have the brainpower right now to sort out whether that was teenage Mysti talking or adult Mysti.

But one night?

Oh, Lord, that she could do. That she *wanted* to do. It would put to rest once and for all those wild imaginings of what being with him might be like. Maybe she'd be sorely disappointed.

But somehow she didn't think so. Anyone who kissed the way he did, who made her react like he did, wasn't going to be anything short of mind-blowing in bed. Beyond her wildest dreams.

She reached out and wrapped her arms around his, leaning her head against the warmth of his shoulder. Just for today she could pretend that he'd chosen her. Because on this particular day, he had.

That would have to be enough. She'd make sure it was enough. And then they had next Saturday together, back out on the lake.

No, don't think beyond today.

"Almost there, Myst. I hope to hell I can make it out of this car."

She giggled, his meaning obvious. "Would it be that bad if you couldn't? There's always the garage."

He didn't say anything for a second, and she could have sworn he stiffened before his lips came down to kiss her temple. "The garage is full of...stuff, so unless you want the whole neighborhood to see you straddling me in the car…"

Heavens. It might be her this time who had trouble getting out. His palm slid higher on her thigh, pushing her shorts up. His fingertips slid beneath them, reaching the elastic of her panties.

"Although I might like that." His voice was low. Husky with desire. "You…straddling me."

She gulped. There was no "might" about it. She wanted to straddle him. Steering wheel at her back. Horn going off with each pump of her hips. "You're making me crazy, Jess."

"Ditto, Myst." His index finger drew another line around the edge of her panties, just as he pulled into a driveway and stopped. One hand cupped her face and turned it toward him, while the other one remained where it was. Then with a sudden movement he pushed underneath her panties, never breaking eye contact. She gasped as the heat of his palm hit her bare skin. He leaned forward, his cheek sliding against hers, stubble adding a delicious sense of friction until he was at her ear. "I can't wait to be. Right. Here."

As he said the words, his thumb edged farther down until he found the core of her.

The sensation took her by storm, and she couldn't stop herself from lifting her hips and pushing into the pressure.

"Yes," he murmured. "Just like that."

He teased her, sliding over her, going even lower, until she wondered if she was going to be able to keep from exploding right here.

Then he withdrew, and the sound of the automatic locks cracked like thunder in the interior of the vehicle. "We need to get out now, before I really do shock my neighbors." He opened his door and climbed out of the car, as she tried to do the same, but her legs were like rubber, shaky and weak when she stood.

His arm went around her waist like at the boat launch, and he walked with her up to the front door of the house, using his key to unlock it and push it open. Then they were inside, and Jesse shoved the door shut with one foot and pivoted her, taking her lips in a smoldering kiss that pushed her into the strong wooden surface behind her.

Fingers undid the fasteners on her bib shortalls and the top of it fell down around her waist, only the side buttons keeping the garment from sliding down completely.

One hand went beneath her shirt, sliding up her torso until he reached her bra. He didn't take it off, but palmed her breast, the stiff peak craving pressure that it didn't get. She arched into him, but his hand was already gone, smoothing down her side until he reached the middle of her back. Her bra went slack two seconds later. Then he returned and this time, he gave her what she wanted, squeezing her nipple between his thumb and forefinger. Her eyes shuddered closed as waves of pleasure crashed through her.

All too soon, he released her, backing up a step and swinging her up into his arms. "Not here. I want you in my bed."

You...straddling me.

His growled words came back to her. And suddenly she knew that's why he wanted her there. He wanted to fulfill a personal fantasy.

Well, that was okay, because her fantasies of him had included every possible angle and position. So she didn't care how he wanted her. She would take him however she could get him.

He entered a room that contained a huge bed.

Kandid's bed? Something in her recoiled

at that thought before she threw the undesirable mental picture into a compartment in her brain and firmly locked the door. Did it really matter?

Not right now.

Holding her suspended over the mattress for a second or two, he finally dropped her onto it, and she squealed as she hit the soft surface. Then he stood over her, watching her. "You are so beautiful, Myst."

He turned and reached into a side drawer and took out a package. Condoms. Of course.

Something else withered inside her.

Stop it, Mysti. Would you rather him not have them?

No, of course not. Besides, the package was new; he'd had to rip open the top before he could withdraw a cellophane packet. She relaxed.

He tossed it on the bed beside her and then hauled his polo shirt over his head in a move that rivaled that of any movie hero, revealing a strong tanned chest and muscular abs. Whoa. That wasn't from a gym. Not with the tan that went along with that six-pack. He must do hard work in the sunshine on his time off.

What kind of work?

Yard work? Log splitting? Did it matter?

No. As long as he got on this bed with her. Right. Now.

She reached for him, but he must have misread her signal because he leaned down and gripped her hands, hauling her into a sitting position instead.

"What's wrong?"

He smiled, the flash of teeth giving a hint of cunning. "Nothing. Nothing at all." He tugged her to her feet, then unbuttoned her pink top, pushing it off her shoulders.

Damn! Her scars. She'd totally forgotten about them. And Lord, she didn't want him seeing them. Not now. Maybe not ever.

She was tempted to snatch her shirt back on, except he would question the move. And she'd be forced to explain.

She didn't want to explain. She just wanted him inside her.

Distract him.

So she undid the side of her shortalls and let them fall. Her bra was next. All she was left in were her lacy peach underwear.

At his intake of breath, she smiled. Yes. She could control how this went down. Could control what he saw or didn't see.

Mysti reached for the button of his khaki shorts and pulled the tab on his zipper, drawing the act out for as long as possible. Gripping the waistband, she tugged them down, watching as he kicked his way out of them. "Did I hear you mention the word *straddle* a little while ago?"

"Hell," he groaned.

She grinned. "Somehow I don't think this will be hell. More like heaven."

Taking his hands, she turned him until his back was to the bed. Then she pushed. Down he went, falling onto the bed with a lot more grace than she had a few minutes ago.

She thought she'd feel more self-conscious being nearly naked in front of him, but his very obvious reaction to her body gave her a courage that surprised her. "So who do you think should go first? You or me? Or should we make it happen together?"

He didn't ask her what she meant. Instead he went along with her. "Together. Definitely."

The wordplay was seductive. As exciting as any physical touch. Maybe more. Because it hinted at what was to come, without spelling it out.

"Okay. Together."

They both peeled down their underwear at the same time and tossed them aside. Jesse was hard and erect and mouthwateringly proportioned. And he would soon be all hers.

At least for an hour or two.

She climbed on top of him, her knees on either side of his thighs, stopping just short of where he jutted in wait. Her body was already a smoldering mass of need.

She wanted to touch him so badly. So she did. Slowly exploring him, amazed at the silky texture of skin that was so very warm in her hands. She pumped him once, twice, three times, watching his face as she did, fascinated by the tightening of muscles and the way his hips jerked up into her grip from time to time.

He allowed her to continue for another minute or two before grabbing her hands and pulling them free. "Enough, Myst."

The words were half croaked as he reached beside him and tore open the condom, rolling it over himself.

"Now," he murmured. "Come here."

She obliged, lifting her hips until she was poised over him. She was already wet and ready, and she slid down over him in one smooth motion, taking all of him.

"Jess…" She was full. So full. Full of him. Full of heat. Full of the need to take them both over the edge. She leaned over to kiss him, but when his hands went to her back in an effort to touch her, she stiffened, then gripped them and carried them up by his head. "Let me do all the work. Just this time."

This time she kissed him, leaving him buried inside her while she remained inert and still. Except for her mouth, which was busy loving him, using her tongue and teeth to show him how much she wanted him. How much she needed him.

Then she started to move, undulating her hips in slow, easy motions that stoked the flame in her belly, urging her to go faster. Somehow she forced herself to maintain her even pace, wanting to draw this out for as long as possible. Never wanting this feeling to end.

He was all she'd dreamed of and more. And far from finally laying her curiosity to rest, she could think of so many other things they could do together. So many opportunities to learn about what he liked. What he didn't.

Unless she was mistaken, he really liked what she was doing.

When his hands came up to grip her hips this time, she didn't stop him. She was quickly moving beyond caring what he did and didn't see right now. Because her senses were wholly tuned in to what was happening in one small part of her body. Angling her a bit farther up, Jesse wrapped an arm around her waist, tilting her until her breasts were within reach of his lips. Then he pulled her into his mouth and the sudden suction on her tender flesh drew a moan from her that went on and on. One of his hands went between her shoulder blades and pressed her closer, and she barely noticed a pause as his fingertips moved over her, then retreated.

"Mysti, I need you." His hips surged forward as she came down on him, and realizing what he wanted, she began to move even faster.

His mouth came up and took hers again, kissing her with a desperation that she felt to her core.

Sitting up, she increased her pace further, her forearms braced on the taut muscles of his chest. Pleasure was winding around her with every thrust of her hips, tightening with each second that passed. His hand slid between them and he found her, sending a reflexive shudder through her, the sensation indescribably wonderful.

Higher and higher she went, her body no longer propelled by her will but by primal instinct. Her eyes closed, all of her focus turning inward as she reached for some distant goal. And then it wasn't distant, but rushing toward her at lightning speed. And when it reached her...

She exploded in a series of convulsions that balled her hands into fists and rolled her eyes in their sockets. From a distance she heard his loud groan, feeling him moving with a speed that seemed superhuman.

And then he joined her in pleasure, Jesse's pace slowing gradually until it was a languorous slide that was pure enjoyment. Her fists released and she relaxed against his chest, her head just beneath his chin.

"That was..." She couldn't finish the sentence, because there were no words that could do justice to what had just happened.

"Yes. I know. For me, too."

She nuzzled him, her lips touching the underside of his jaw before coming up to tease him with kisses across his cheek, planting one last one on his chin. Then she laid her head back down.

His fingertips trailed across her lower back, the sensation half tickly, half soothing, and she allowed her eyes to drift shut, enjoying his ministrations. His touch swirled higher, and she sighed.

"You're going to make me go to sleep."

"No. Not quite yet," he growled.

Not yet? Did he mean he wanted her again?

He chuckled as if reading her mind. Then his fingers paused at her shoulder like they had done earlier, and with a rush of awareness she realized where he was. When she tried to pull away from his touch, he held her still, his fingers still exploring.

"What is this?" He sat up, and he leaned to the side as if he was going to look, but she stopped him, shaking her head as swift tears came to her eyes.

"No, Jesse. Don't. Please don't."

CHAPTER TEN

THERE WAS SOMETHING in her shaky plea that held him frozen for a second or two.

"Let me. Please."

Mysti's chin went up, but this time she didn't stop him from angling her sideways so he could look. His jaw clenched, all the memories of what they'd just shared obliterated when a series of thick angry scars came into view. Scars that riddled her left shoulder blade and sprayed in an arc that coated a good part of her back on that side. Most of it, though, was on the shoulder that he'd seen her roll more than once.

He repeated his earlier question. "What is this?"

For several seconds there was silence, then she said, "I was hit by shrapnel from an IED."

Words were stuck in his throat for several long seconds.

"Damn. Did I hurt you? When we were…"

"No. I don't notice it for the most part."

He didn't think that was quite the truth. "Did this happen when you were in Joronha?"

"Yes. A good friend of mine was killed by it. I survived because I was farther away from it when it blew." Her eyes closed. "And her…her body blocked some of the blast."

Shock and horror washed over him at her words.

"I'm so sorry. Why didn't you say something to me before?"

"Why?" She shifted around to face him. "What could you have said or done? Or maybe you wouldn't have wanted to make love to me if you'd known how bad it was."

"No." He took hold of her shoulders, trying to keep his own emotions under wraps. He could not even imagine what she had gone through. What she had endured afterward. "Nothing could have stopped what happened between us. It's been building for a long time."

She gave him a slight smile. "Yes. It has."

He separated himself from her, then tugging her with him, he moved until he was leaning against the headboard, with Mysti resting on his chest. "Do you want to tell me about it?"

She shrugged, and he wondered for a minute if that meant no. But then she started talking.

"Like I said earlier, Laura was a friend of mine. She was in my squad. I found out about a year into our deployment there that she'd become pregnant. If her commander had found out, she'd have been shipped straight home. So she hid it until she could decide what she wanted to do, asking me not to tell anyone. She said the father was a soldier she'd hooked up with over the period of a few months, but that it had never been serious." She sighed. "I don't know who it was. But I kept my promise and held on to her secret. I told no one. Not her commander. Not her other friends. Not even her parents after she died. I didn't want anything tarnishing her service record, not that it should have mattered. You're the first person I've ever shared that secret with." She pulled down an audible breath. "Anyway, we were on the way to see a local midwife we'd heard about to see how far along she was."

Her breathing quickened, and she plucked at the bedspread beside her. "We didn't make it that far. We were walking over ground we assumed had been cleared. I was ahead of her and she was following a small distance behind. I thought she was walking in my footsteps. Then something behind me exploded and before I could turn around, I was knocked off my feet by the blast, and felt a searing pain in my back that I immediately recognized from treating so many other soldiers.

"Someone had planted an IED. When I could finally sit up, I saw blood on the ground where I'd fallen and when I looked back…" She gave a visible swallow. "I couldn't even recognize what was left of her. I remember yelling her name, then everything went black."

"God. I'm so sorry, Myst."

"They said I woke up in the field hospital screaming, although the details of the first several weeks after being hit are pretty foggy. They evidently spent quite a bit of time picking pieces of metal out of me.

"After I healed, I couldn't work. Couldn't sleep. I was a mess. I kept thinking if I'd forced her to tell someone she was pregnant, we wouldn't have been sneaking away to see that midwife, wouldn't have been breaking the rules about going out in singles or pairs." Her eyes closed for several seconds, then reopened, revealing deep green wells of pain. "They ended up shipping me back to the States to go through counseling for what they said was PTSD."

"That's when you decided to get out of the military."

"Yes. I decided I was enough of a mess that I wouldn't be very effective back out on the field. Not in a month. Not in six months. So I decided to get out. I had a medical discharge, and they forgave the rest of the service time I had left for my medical degree. I thought home—Forgotten Point—might be a place of healing, which is why I applied for that three-month position at Serenity Regional."

"And has it been a place of healing?"

"I think so. At least until Larry died." She shook her head. "I treated so many wounded soldiers. I'd get them patched up and they would do well. I thought they would get better. Except some of them didn't. Some of them died from unforeseen complications. An aneurysm. A blood clot. One committed suicide a month after he was declared fit for duty."

"Hell. Did Larry bring back those memories for you?"

Her face crumpled. "We'd declared him fit, Jess. Then he died."

His arm tightened around her, a wave of

compassion swamping him and threatening to pull him under. Hell, he'd had no idea she'd even suffered an injury, much less carried the guilt of her friend's accident, or of other soldiers' deaths, along with her. And although his medical specialty brought death with it on a regular basis, it was more the natural order of things. Elderly patients passed away. But to see young men and women suffer and die from something as senseless as a conflict between nations… It was hard to fathom how anyone dealt with it. And being a medical professional in that setting had to be traumatic for all of them.

"Larry *was* fit, Mysti. As fit as anyone could have guessed at the time. You can't always predict blood clots. Or heart rhythm episodes. Or even if you'll be hit by a car walking across the street. He was incredibly happy to be at that tournament. And he got help almost immediately. We were both on the scene."

"I know. I don't really know why it's hitting me as hard as it is."

"I can understand that." He paused, asking a question he hadn't realized had been forming. "You said being home has helped in some ways. Does that mean you're going to stay in Forgotten Point after the three months are up?"

A couple of beats passed. "I actually haven't decided yet. I thought I'd give myself this time to see how I fit here." She smiled. "So ask me again in another month or so."

His heart froze in his chest. She hadn't exactly said no to staying. But she hadn't said yes, either. Wasn't this why he'd decided not to let Sally be around her too much? And now he'd had her in his bed. Had asked her to go back out on the boat next weekend. What had he been thinking?

He decided to ignore his misgivings. She hadn't said she was leaving. Just said she needed to see if she fit here. What if she did? What then? Could he risk it?

His fingers teased the silky skin of her arm, feeling her snuggle closer as he did. Why did he need to think a month or two ahead? Why couldn't he simply enjoy her being back? Enjoy getting to know her again? He had a feeling she hadn't told anyone else about her wounds except maybe her mother.

"Does your mom know what happened to you?"

She immediately tensed. "No. And please

don't tell her. I just haven't been ready to say anything. To anyone."

So she'd chosen to share that information with him first? He thrust down the pleasure. Not really. Only because he'd felt the skin back there and had wanted to see what it was. She'd actually tried to stop him at first. But once he'd seen it, she'd shared her story as if relieved to have someone finally know about it.

He was glad it was him. No matter what the reason.

"Thank you for telling me. It'll go no further."

"Thanks." Her stiff muscles loosened back up, her fingers coming up to touch his face. "You've got stubble coming up."

He smiled. "Does it bother you?"

"No. I like it. Loved feeling it scrape across my cheek earlier."

His fingers encircled her wrist, and he drew her palm to his lips, kissing the center of it. "I'm glad."

"I really like Sally. She's a sweet girl."

He forced himself not to react to the words. "Thank you. I'll admit, I'm pretty partial to her myself."

"As you should be." Her index finger traced his lips. "I'm glad I told you about what happened. It's like a weight has been lifted. More than with the counselors and treatment programs, even, since I opted not to disclose Laura's pregnancy. They couldn't really help me with my guilt, as they didn't understand the cause of it. But knowing you think I'm not a monster for keeping it a secret helps."

"Never. You're a kind, compassionate woman who suffered a horrific loss and a terrible injury. But thank God you're still here. I'm not sure I can imagine a world without Mysti North in it."

It was true. Jesse couldn't imagine Mysti not being somewhere. He'd grieved Kandid's death, but not the way a husband should have. He'd grieved more that Sally wouldn't grow up with her mother. Grieved that he hadn't always been able to love his wife the way he should have. In the end, he hadn't cheated on her, but he also hadn't been a stellar example of what love and marriage should look like. Maybe that's why Kandid had looked elsewhere for comfort.

And worse, maybe he'd never really gotten over a certain kiss in a storm. Whether his difficulty expressing emotions with Kandid had been due to guilt or because that kiss had triggered some deeper emotion in him, he wasn't sure. And exploring that in depth would only bring him more pain. More guilt. Maybe that's why he still hadn't been able to part with the bulk of Kandid's stuff. It was stored in the garage. His thought was that he could let Sally look through it when she got older and pick out what she wanted to keep, and then he'd get rid of the rest.

Really? Was that the real reason?

That was something else he wasn't going to examine right now with another woman in his arms. A woman who...

He gulped. Did he love her?

Too soon. Way too soon. Mysti hadn't even committed to staying in Forgotten Point yet.

He could wait. Let her get her footing over these three months. And if she did that and wanted to stay?

Well, then they might just have to sit down and have a long talk.

But for right now, he was going to do his best to live in the present. To enjoy the here and now with her.

He half rolled onto his side, one leg sliding between hers. Looking down at her, with her flushed face, her mussed hair, and eyes that were bright and alive, parts of him began to come back to life, nudging at her thigh.

Her eyes widened as if realizing what was happening. "Dr. Grove, you appear to have a growing problem."

"Problem?" He chuckled. "Where you see a problem, I see an opportunity."

"Oh, I'm not complaining. And I kind of liked that straddle thing."

His flesh reacted with even more enthusiasm. "Yes, I liked that, too. But this time I think I'd like to be the driver." He rolled the rest of the way on top of her, supporting most of his weight on his elbows. "And I mean that both figuratively and literally."

When she arched against him, he couldn't hold back a low groan.

"I really like the sound of that." She grinned up at him. "Both figuratively. And literally."

Jesse hesitated before picking up the phone several days later. But he'd promised himself he would not let what had happened that night change who they were at work. They were colleagues. Professionals. Doctors often called on each other to run things by them. And this was important.

So he turned his cell phone over and found her number.

Mysti picked up on the third ring. "Hi, Jess."

Of course she knew who it was. She would have entered his number into her phone. But she could delete it just as easily on her way out of town.

Where the hell had that thought come from?

"Hey. How busy is your schedule?"

"It's not packed. What's up?"

Jesse pulled the file closer. "I have a seventy-four-year-old patient who's down in the ER right now with a compound fracture to her radius. I'm about to head over there."

"Okay. Do you want me to take a look?"

"Do you mind? I would say this is normal, but the attending says she's insisting she slipped in the shower, and when she went to catch herself on the wall, she heard a sharp snap and the next thing she knew the bone was protruding from her forearm."

"Osteoporotic?"

"No, that's what worries me. She had a compression fracture to her L2 vertebra a while back after a fall from a ladder. At the time it seemed like a normal injury, but I ordered a bone density test just to be sure I wasn't missing something. There was some expected loss of bone mass but not enough to classify it as osteoporosis or even osteopenia." Osteopenia was a precursor to more serious loss of bone mass and would have given him cause to keep a closer eye on it.

"Snapping that bone would have taken quite a bit of pressure, then. Unless she actually fell with all of her weight on it…"

"I know."

"What's the patient's name?"

"Gertrude Evans."

"Wait." There was a pause. "As in Mrs. Evans who taught us at Forgotten Point High?"

"Yep. Can you meet me in the ER? She's being admitted and the attending… Well, let's just say he's not the most patient doc on the planet."

Jesse didn't like talking about his colleagues like that, but he also tended to be protective of his patients and wanted them with doctors who were good at handling the intricacies of emotion that sometimes came with aging. Mrs. Evans could be direct and would not take well to someone talking down to her like she was a child.

"Got it. I'm on my way there now."

While his receptionist phoned some of

his afternoon patients to see if they could shuffle his appointments around, he headed down the hallway toward the main building. By the time he got to Mrs. Evans's room, he found Mysti already there talking to her. There was no sign of Eric Porter, the attending physician.

Mysti turned to him, trying to hide a smile. "She said she already fired the last guy."

"Yes, I did." His patient was holding her arm, which was already covered with a layer of sterile gauze to keep it clean. Despite her obvious pain, there was still fire in her eyes. "He didn't understand the meaning of 'Talk to me like I can understand.'"

The same plastic shoes she'd worn to his office over a month ago were on the ground next to the exam bed. There were a couple of spots of blood on them this time. Something about that made his gut tighten. "Tell me what happened. I know you already told Dr. Porter, but I want to hear the story."

Something about standing beside Mysti as Gertrude Evans explained what had happened felt good and right. He'd expected to feel some sort of awkwardness between them, but it was as if they'd reverted back to a time in the past when they'd been good friends, something he hadn't felt since that kiss in his car fifteen years ago. It was as if everything that had been turned on its head back then had been righted by the night they'd spent together.

"So you started to fall, your arm hit the grab bar on the way down and then you caught yourself with that same arm."

She nodded.

So either Porter had been in a hurry and hadn't gotten her story straight, or she'd been minimizing what had happened out of fear someone would want to take her farm away from her. He could see how that kind of fall could have resulted in the injury. Striking the arm hard enough against the bar could have fractured the bone, then catching herself could have pushed it through the skin. When he glanced at Mysti, she nodded as if reading his thoughts.

But he still wanted to check something out.

"You remember that MRI you had with your compression fracture? I'd like to repeat that with your arm."

"Okay. What are you looking for?"

"I'm not as worried as I was when Dr. Porter first called me, but I'd like to rule out a lesion on the bone causing the fracture."

"In other words, cancer."

Mrs. Evans had never liked things to be wrapped in pretty boxes. She wanted the ugly truth no matter what it was. "Yes. I just want to make sure nothing weakened your radius and made it more likely to fracture."

She eyed Mysti. "And you'll be the one fixing my arm?"

"I'm a surgeon, so I could in a pinch. But I think I'd like to see you with someone who specializes in orthopedics. I'm simply here to keep Dr. Grove in line." She smiled at the woman, who laughed.

"I always said he needed someone to do that."

Jesse read something behind the older woman's words that he hoped Mysti didn't hear. But if she did, she didn't show it, just kept on smiling.

"I'll get your MRI set up and see how soon we can get that arm fixed." He called the order in, and thankfully they were going to be able to get her in almost immediately.

Five minutes later, Gertrude was being wheeled out of the room and headed for the elevator.

Mysti and Jesse followed her out.

"Sorry for calling you over. What I heard

over the phone didn't sound quite as clear-cut as Gertrude explained it."

"No reason to be sorry, and I agree with you. I also agree with getting an MRI just to be sure there's no underlying cause for that bone to be weakened. Care if I sit with you as she gets her scan? I always did like Mrs. Evans as a teacher."

"So did I. And I could certainly use some good news on this case."

He didn't have to say he was referring to Larry. The quick feel of her hand squeezing his before letting go told him she understood how he felt, because she felt the same.

The MRI didn't take long, and since he'd asked for the scans to be read immediately so they knew how to proceed on the surgical repair, the radiologist met them there.

The group peered at the slides as they came off the computer, with Deke Phillips frowning as he studied each one. "I'll give them a closer look after I finish my day, but I'm not seeing any obvious problem areas in that bone or in her other arm. If there's a lesion, I'm just not spotting it. So I say go ahead with surgery and get the break repaired."

They stood and shook hands. "Thanks, I appreciate you coming down."

Deke laughed. "Not a problem. I had her in school. So I know better than to do a sloppy job. She'd call me out on it."

Yes, she would. He imagined there were quite a few folks in Forgotten Point who'd had Mrs. Evans as an English teacher. And Deke was right. He would be called out, in exactly the same way she'd called out Dr. Porter.

They gave her the news together, letting her know that the orthopedic surgeon was already scrubbing up to repair her arm.

"Is he any good?"

"I'd say you'd give him an A if he were in your class."

Gertrude reached out and grabbed Mysti's hand with her good one. "I'm going to hold you to keeping this one in line. He needs it."

With that, she was wheeled away yet again, leaving Jesse and Mysti staring after her.

When they looked at each other, they both burst out laughing. "She is too funny." Mysti scrubbed a palm under one of her eyes to blot the tears. "You were right, you know. We did need some good news. And I think we just got it."

"Yes," he murmured. "I think we just did."

CHAPTER ELEVEN

MYSTI WAS EXCITED about their boating trip today. Even though they'd seen each other at work, a full week had passed since she'd spent the night with him. And although they hadn't slept together since then or talked about what had happened, she remembered with a shiver how he'd reached for her again and again in the middle of the night. He had fixed her a delicious breakfast before driving her home the next day. And he'd been friendly ever since, with a hint of almost flirty banter between them at the hospital when no one was around.

The case with Gertrude Evans had seemed to solidify that easy rapport. And boy, she could get used to this.

It was what she'd once dreamed about having with him. The fact that he'd married Kandid was something she couldn't go back and change, and she certainly didn't want to ask him about it. He'd obviously loved her deeply or he wouldn't have married her.

But widowed people did remarry. And she was pretty sure none of those people thought their new partner was second best or somehow less than the spouse who'd died. It was just different. Maybe it was the same way parents could love more than one child.

Who'd said anything about love?

Not her. She was just going to keep things loose and easy. She was still sorting out how she felt about returning to Forgotten Point. But she had to admit, she was feeling better and better about being here.

And she was looking forward to being with him. To getting to know Sally a little better. She'd finally gotten to see what being with Jesse in a more intimate setting was like.

It had been wonderful and amazing. And when he'd turned her onto her stomach and traced her scars, he'd brought her to tears, loving her as he kissed those marks one at a time. It had made her feel wholly accepted. Wholly cared about. Wholly...

Nope. She was going to stop right there.

She glanced at her watch. He was due to pick her up in just a few minutes. She quickly pulled on her bathing suit, the first time she'd worn one since her injury. She turned around to look at the scarring in the mirror. Her strap covered part of it up, but the scooped back showed off more than she would have wanted, once upon a time. But it would just be her and Sally and Jess. And if his daughter asked what had happened to her, she would simply respond that she'd gotten hurt.

She slid on shorts and a loose gauzy top that was long enough to act as a cover-up for her suit if they ended up using an inner tube or skis. But she didn't care about any of that. She just wanted to be with him. They could have gone cycling for all she cared. But Jesse had said he wanted to start using his boat more, for Sally's sake. And for his.

She shoved her feet into sandals and tucked a pair of water shoes into her tote bag in case they ended up getting out and wading in some shallows.

Her phone rang, and she glanced at the readout. It was her mom.

"Hi, how did Brutus's appointment go?"

Their vet was open on Saturday mornings, and her mother had wanted the Saint Bernard scheduled for a recheck. "It went fine. I told you I wouldn't need help. He jumped in and out of the car like a champ."

"Great." She'd been a little worried about that, but her mother had insisted on taking the dog on her own, especially once she'd heard that Mysti had plans for today.

"I'm so glad you're going out. Jesse's seemed kind of sad ever since Kandid's death."

She tried not to think of all the pictures of Kandid that had been scattered throughout his house when she was over there. There weren't any in the bedroom. But the living room had more than enough framed snapshots to make up for that. The pictures had made her tense when she saw happy smiling faces in all of them, but of course Jesse wouldn't throw those away—or even put them in storage. He'd loved Kandid. And she was Sally's mom.

Mysti frowned. "I'm sure he was. She was his wife for quite a while, Mom."

"I know that. But people do fall in love again."

Please don't ruin this.

The fact that she herself had just thought the exact same thing didn't help. Those pictures meant nothing. Right? Not even the one of Jesse gazing lovingly at Kandid while she held a baby Sally in her arms.

"You didn't," she pointed out.

Her mom laughed. "I know. But your dad and I had been married for almost forty years."

"I don't think there's a time limit on love." Her voice came out a little harsher than she meant for it to. "Sorry. I just don't want you making a big deal over this. Jess and I are friends. We've been friends since we were kids."

"Yes. I know."

The way her mother said it confirmed some of her suspicions about what her mom knew or didn't know about her feelings for Jesse all those years ago. At least she prayed that was what this was about. She hoped to hell she wasn't giving off some kind of weird pheromones that told her mom she had her sights set on Jesse. Because she didn't want to do that. Didn't want to rush into anything. Especially not after everything they'd both been through in their lives. Jesse had Kandid's death to recover from. And she had Laura's and her own injuries to get over. Maybe she was just grabbing at life a little too fast.

Her doorbell rang at that second, thankfully.

"Mom, I have to go. They're here for me."

"Okay, have fun. And forget everything I said. I'm just being a hopeless romantic."

Mysti sighed, sorry that she'd snapped. "I know you are. It's one of the many things I love about you. And I'm glad Brutus's appointment went well. I'll call you when I get home. And I'll have my cell phone on me if you need me for anything."

"Go. I'll be fine. But I promise to call if there are any problems."

"Thanks. Talk to you tonight."

With that she hung up and grabbed her tote bag, hurrying to the door. She wondered if she should have packed a lunch. But they hadn't gotten a chance to eat the last one, because of Larry, and they hadn't talked about how long they'd be out on the water. Maybe he didn't mean for this to be an all-day excursion.

Pulling open the door, she smiled when she saw Jesse there holding his daughter's hand. He'd done an admirable job putting Sally's hair into two neat pigtails, pink ribbons tied in a bow on each side.

"Hi," she said, giving him a nervous smile.

"Hi, yourself. I think I'm a few minutes early, so if you need more time…"

"Nope, I'm ready." She stepped out, closing the door on her little rental cottage. It sat

at the back of a local farmer's property. He'd
originally built it to house his adult children
and grandkids, but even the grandkids were
now grown up. So Mysti's mom had talked
him into letting her rent it for as long as she
was here. She was pretty sure the farmer
was just glad to have someone in it to keep
it clean. And fortunately, it had come fully
furnished, which was a huge help. Even if it
hadn't, Mysti was used to soldiers' quarters
and tent housing. So this was like a luxury
hotel in comparison.

"How's Gertrude doing? Have you heard?"

"She's great. Doing too much with her
arm in a sling, but that's Gertrude."

A sense of relief went through her. "I'm
so glad."

She then smiled and stooped to look Jesse's daughter in the eye. "Hi, Sally. Are you
ready to get back on the boat?"

"Yes! Dad said I might be able to sit with
him on a tube."

"A tube?"

Jesse glanced at her. "I brought some skis
and some water things, but I told her maybe.
I didn't promise. I didn't want to commit you
to driving the boat if you didn't want to."

"I think that sounds like fun. I'd be happy
to, especially since I forgot to ask my mom

about my skis. Anyway, I can go nice and slow."

He reached and gave her hand a squeeze as she stood back up. "Thanks. So can I."

They shared a look that made her smile.

If Sally noticed the exchange or the quick touch, she didn't say anything. But it sent an unexpected burst of warmth through Mysti. She was glad things weren't weird between them, but was also kind of weirded out that they weren't. Her mouth twitched. So by using *weird* twice in a sentence, did it act like a double negative, meaning things really *were* weird?

Ugh. Too much thinking. Again.

She walked toward the car, Jesse and Sally behind her. The boat and trailer were already hooked up to his truck, so they wouldn't have to stop and do that. When something brushed the skin of her left shoulder, she flinched before realizing it was Jesse.

"Sorry. I was just going to say, I like your blouse."

The white cover-up was scooped in the back like her swimsuit and probably still revealed some of her scars when she moved. She hadn't checked, but was glad that it didn't bother him.

It certainly hadn't seemed to last week.

"It's okay. It just startled me." She opened the back door for Sally and waited for her to climb in. "I didn't pack a lunch. I wasn't sure what your plans were."

"No plans. And I packed one again this time. I seem to remember you had cold fried chicken on the menu, so I brought that."

"I love it."

She leaned into the truck and got Sally buckled in, tweaking her nose as she did, causing the child to laugh.

More warmth bubbled inside her. This little girl was absolutely precious.

She realized it might seem like she was taking over with Sally, but Jesse didn't seem to mind. In fact, he smiled at her when she closed the door. "I hope it was okay for me to buckle her in."

"Yes. It was more than okay."

She swallowed down an unexpected rush of emotion, moving away to get into the front passenger seat.

Twenty minutes later, they were back across the bridge and at the landing they'd used for the fishing tournament. The place looked oddly abandoned, with only three boat trailers parked in the lot. A week ago, Larry was out there fishing and planning on taking home that trophy for the third time in a row.

How things changed in such a short space of time. What had he said in that exam room?

None of us knows how long we'll travel this earth.

Larry certainly hadn't known. Neither had Laura. Or Kandid, for that matter.

So shouldn't she try to make the most of every moment?

Yes. She should. And part of that was allowing herself to enjoy today for what it was. There was no need to worry about what tomorrow might bring or the next day. Sometimes it was better to live in the here and now.

And for today, at least, she meant to do just that.

The sound of screaming eclipsed the rumble of the boat motor and Jesse turned quickly to look before smiling broadly. Sally and Mysti were huddled together on a towable tube he'd purchased just for the occasion. In his mind, it reminded him of a small inflatable boat and seemed safer than an inner tube, which had no bottom to it.

Mysti's arms were around Sally, despite

the bulk of both of their life jackets, and from what he could tell, his daughter was having the time of her life. He'd already taken his turn with her while Mysti steered the boat, and she'd insisted that she wanted to ride with Mysti next. A momentary flash of worry had been quickly quashed.

Today was a day for fun. Not worrying. If this had been one of Sally's friends, he wouldn't be sitting here stymied by the idea of her getting too attached or anything else.

Maybe he should be more worried about *him* getting too attached to her.

Because from everything he sensed inside himself, that was more than just a possibility. It was already a reality. But Mysti seemed happy in Forgotten Point, despite her earlier words about not being sure if she'd extend her stay after her three months were up. He hadn't felt in her that frantic need to leave that she'd had the day of their high school kiss and afterward.

He waved, then turned back to navigating the boat. It had been quiet on the lake today, probably because of how busy it had been last week. And since Sally was here and there were no plans for her to spend the night at his mom's house, there would be no sleepovers or anything else with Mysti. So it took away some of that pressure. Not that there wasn't part of him that wanted her. Had badly wanted her all week.

Not going to think about it.

Not going to think about how right it looked for his daughter to be held by a woman other than Kandid. He made a wide turn so that they could go over the boat's wake, not that there was much of one at this slow rate of speed. But that was his daughter back there, and he wasn't taking any chances, no matter how much she yelled for him to "make waves."

He'd made enough waves already with what had happened with Mysti last weekend. But those waves had been wild and wonderful, and he hadn't given a thought to speed. He'd wanted to go as fast as he could. Until he couldn't go any more. It had been the night of a lifetime.

He rolled his eyes. And there he went again. Thinking.

Changing directions and circling to the left, he gave Sally another small wake, then he throttled down and slowed to a stop. He didn't want her or Mysti getting seasick by keeping them out there for too long. It had already been twenty minutes, and his grumbling stomach told him it was about time to take a lunch break.

Letting the boat drift toward the center of the lake, he slowly reeled in the tube until they were within reach of the teak swim platform at the back of the boat. Jesse held the rope while Mysti handed Sally over, setting her on the platform. He put her in the boat and told her to go sit down, then he held out a hand for Mysti. She took it and stepped onto the platform, passing a little too close to him. On purpose?

Her saucy smile said yes, and he grabbed her hand and tugged it until she was flush against him. "Sorry. Looks like you tripped." He grinned at her and then let her go.

"More like I was tripped by a certain someone."

She stepped onto the boat, walking toward the seat next to Sally while he hauled the float inside and lashed it to the aft side so it wouldn't blow away. "I'm going to move toward shore and set the anchor. I don't know if anyone else is hungry, but I am."

"Me! Me!" Sally raised her hand, her pink nose reminding him that he'd probably better reapply her sunscreen.

They set up the canopy for shade, and Jesse flipped up the little tables that were attached to each of the seats. He then passed out plates and containers of food.

"I am going to be so spoiled," Mysti remarked. "You haven't let me do anything today."

"You've made my daughter happy. That's huge."

"We had fun, didn't we, Sally?"

"Yes! I want Mysti to always come on all of our trips!"

His insides tightened before he forced them to release. "We'll have to see what happens."

Mysti nodded as if thanking him for pulling her out of the fire. That worried him a bit. He wasn't going to pressure her or force her to make decisions she wasn't ready to make, but he did need to think about Sally. As much as he'd thought about Mysti being like any of Sally's other friends, it wasn't exactly true.

But it was still early days. If Mysti disappeared out of their lives right now, Sally wouldn't really suffer. Because there hadn't been a big emotional investment made in her.

Except by him.

But he was a grown-up. He'd handled

her leaving once before. He could handle it again.

Maybe he could think of a way to put some feelers out. She'd definitely been flirting with him earlier. Of course, he had been just as guilty of playing games.

But a time was coming when he was going to want something a little more substantial than games.

He sat down across from them and ate, while Sally talked about school and her friends. And she commented on how much she liked her teacher.

"I'm glad you like her," Mysti said. "Ms. Lewis and I went to high school together."

"She said you did. She's really nice. She lets us pet frogs."

Mysti laughed. "She had a bearded dragon as a pet when we were in school. I helped her feed it."

"She has one of those now, too. He's our class mascot. His name is Snuffles and we help take care of him."

"Wow," she said. "I guess some things never change."

Jesse tensed again at that before deciding he was reading too much into her words. It wasn't a warning from fate. She was just talking about a friend and her lizard.

And he could say the same of kissing her again in the rain. Some things never did change. Or maybe they did. Because watching his daughter laughing with Mysti had done his heart good. He and Kandid had rarely laughed with their daughter. Oh, they each did in their own way, but when they were all together, there'd often been an underlying tension that was hard to overcome.

He'd asked himself a question the other night, and maybe it was time to own the truth. He loved Mysti.

Maybe he always had and just hadn't realized it. Hadn't let himself admit it. Even in school.

But by admitting it now, wasn't he setting himself up for heartache all over again? Maybe. Probably. But at least he wouldn't always wonder what would have happened if he'd told her the truth about how he felt. Not in the past. But right now.

Maybe he would. He'd give it a little more time. He could ask her out on an actual date. One where they dressed up and went out to dinner and where they talked like they had after they'd made love. She'd shared stuff with him that she said she'd never told anyone else. That had to count for something, didn't it?

He really hoped so.

Mysti got up from her seat and picked up the trash from their lunch, disposing of it in the trash bag they'd brought with them. She gave him a smile, the sides of her nose crinkling in a way he remembered fondly. And he didn't think she'd rolled her shoulder one single time today.

He caught at her hand, releasing it when she turned toward him. He still needed to be careful about displays of affection around Sally. "How is it?" He nodded in the direction of her injuries.

"Hmm… I don't think it's bothered me at all today. Maybe it's from all the stretching on the float."

"I'm glad."

"Yeah. Me, too." She smiled, touching the back of his hand with her index finger and letting it slide against his skin for a second. "Thanks for inviting me."

"I'm really glad you could come."

She pulled in a deep breath and let it out with what sounded like sincere contentment. "So am I."

They stayed on the boat another hour or so before Sally started to get restless. "Ready to call it a day?" Jesse asked.

He didn't want to. He could stay out here

forever, but they were going to have to go in sometime.

"I guess we should. Besides, I told my mom I would call her when I got in."

Mysti didn't sound any more anxious to go than he did. And that made him happy.

They made their way back to the boat launch and winched it out of the water. "Do you mind stopping by the house to drop off the boat first? Turning around on your narrow lane was a little challenging this morning."

"That's a great idea."

All too soon they were in front of his house. He unhitched the boat. "Anyone need to make a bathroom break?"

"It probably wouldn't be a bad idea." She unstrapped the float from inside the boat. "Where do you want this?" she asked as he gathered up the picnic stuff and life jackets.

"We'll just dump all of it in the garage. I'll rinse them off tomorrow."

They walked toward the house with their arms loaded with stuff. And he unlocked the front door for Sally, so she could go to the restroom.

He set all the stuff on the ground. "I'll go around and open the garage door for you."

"Sounds good. I'll wait here."

* * *

Mysti smiled to herself as she waited for Jesse. Today had been...wonderful. And it just went to prove that the pictures in his house were just reminders. Remnants of the past that didn't hold a real place in his heart anymore. A part of her felt like he'd proved that today.

God, when he'd pulled her to him on that swim platform, she'd thought her heart was going to burst. It was like a dream. One she never wanted to wake up from.

This was the same Jesse she'd wanted back in high school. The one who made little comments only the two of them would understand. The one who kissed her until she was breathless. The one who...loved her.

She swallowed. Could he ever?

She'd been devastated once before; could she risk her heart again? This time with a more mature Jesse? Maybe one who realized love wasn't all about looks or popularity, but about two people who genuinely liked each other.

She heard a sound from inside the garage, and the door slowly rolled up, the click-click-click of the mechanism seeming to echo the ticking of her heart.

She picked up the float while Jesse came

and grabbed an armful of the other stuff. As he came nearer he kissed her softly on the lips. She smiled. "Where's Sally?"

"Somewhere she can't see."

"Mmm… In that case…" She leaned forward and kissed him a bit harder. "Okay, back to work. Where do you want this exactly?"

"Just in the middle of the floor. It's kind of cluttered in there right now."

"That's okay."

She ducked inside, letting her eyes adjust to the light. Then she glanced around as she found a place to set the float. Jesse dumped one load, then went out for another.

Something on the wall caught her attention, and her heart lurched. There was a cheerleading skirt and shirt in a clear garment bag hanging on a hook. And there were clothes racks. With dresses. And shoes. And sparkly formals.

Kandid's stuff. He hadn't gotten rid of it.

Everywhere she looked she saw more of it. A dressing table. A tall vase. Knickknacks. She turned toward the wall on the other side of the space and a strange pressure built in her head. There was a large portrait of Jesse, Kandid and a much younger

Sally sitting on a painter's easel. It looked similar to one she'd seen inside the house.

But this was so much more than some pictures on the wall in the living room.

It looked like a shrine. A shrine to Jesse's dead wife.

Nausea gathered in her stomach, frothing around the edges and threatening to find the nearest exit. Jesse came back inside and somehow…from somewhere within the depths of her, she managed to dredge up a semblance of a smile. "I'll just wait outside."

"Do you need to use the restroom?"

"Nope. I'll be home in just a few minutes. Thanks though."

She went outside and waited by the car.

How was she going to pretend that everything was normal all that way? Because those "few minutes" were going to take forever. No one kept all their loved one's things for that many years unless they were finding it impossible to let them go. Look at her mom, who refused to date or even look at another man, because she was still so desperately in love with her husband. She hadn't thought that was weird, so why would it be weird for Jesse to hold on to Kandid?

Mysti closed her eyes, trying to keep the

pain at bay. He'd made love to her as if she'd meant something.

But then again, he'd kissed her in high school as if she'd meant something, too. That had proved to be a lie, because he'd gone ahead and married Kandid.

Was sleeping with her just as much of a lie? She pressed her hand to her mouth to hold in a low, tortured cry as a thought erupted from somewhere inside her. Had she simply been a placeholder for Kandid while she'd been in his bed?

The evidence in that garage said so. Said he'd just needed someone to let off some steam with. And all that flirting on the boat?

Why would it be anything different? If he was ready to move on, he would have donated Kandid's things—or at least her clothes—to charity, wouldn't he? She couldn't bear to go inside the house right now and see all of those other pictures again.

Sally and Jesse came back out. "Sally wants to know if you want to get ice cream on the way?"

The nausea returned full force. "Oh, honey, I'm sorry but I can't. I promised my mom I would check on Brutus and see how he's doing. I think I told you about how he got hurt."

Jesse tilted his head. "You sure?"

"Yes. If you'll drop me off, you two can go. I'm beat. And like I said, I promised my mom I'd call. But thanks for today. I had so much fun."

It was true; she had. But God, she wished he'd never opened up that garage door.

And if he hadn't? And she'd slept with him again, confessed that she loved him, like she'd been toying with? How big of a fool would that have made her?

Kandid was dead, and she wasn't coming back. But Mysti couldn't—she *wouldn't*—compete with a ghost. Yes, widowers married again, but they didn't usually choose someone from their past. Someone they'd already passed over once in favor of their late spouse.

What was she going to say if he asked her out again? If he pulled her toward him?

Oh God. She was going to have to leave town again. She couldn't stay here. Not after this.

Her only consolation was that her job wasn't permanent and that she'd already told Jesse she wasn't sure if she was staying afterward. So if she told him that she'd gotten a job offer somewhere else and had decided to take it?

That would be a lie.

Except that technically, it wouldn't. She'd already spoken to a friend from Doctors Without Borders right before coming back to Forgotten Point. He'd told her to call him if she ever decided to do something different with her life. Something that would do a lot of good in a lot of different places instead of just one. He'd give her a job immediately. She'd wondered if coming back here was a mistake. And it looked like she'd just gotten her answer. It was.

Because there was no way she could bear it if Jesse told her the truth: that he was still in love with Kandid and that was never going to change.

Somehow she got in the truck and made the appropriate small talk as they drove to her house. A million thoughts and plans were racing through her head. And they all centered on escape. Escape from this car. Escape from this situation. Escape from Forgotten Point.

But her ideas were slowly crystallizing into something solid. Something she could hang on to until she was able to leave.

First, she was going to call her friend and see if he'd been serious about his offer. If that didn't pan out, she was going to give the hospital whatever notice they required and live off her savings until she could actually find something else. She had no doubt that she'd be able to by the time her notice was up. Trauma surgeons with her experience weren't exactly a dime a dozen. How much trauma work had she actually seen in this small hospital, anyway? Besides the trauma to her heart, that was.

They pulled into her narrow gravel lane and drove the rest of the distance to the cottage in silence. She'd given up trying to talk during the last couple of minutes. Jesse had glanced at her a couple of times, frowning slightly, but didn't ask any questions. For which she was more grateful than he would ever know. He stopped in front of the house, and she was out of her seat belt in a flash, hand on the release for the door. "Thank you again for everything. It was fun."

"I'll walk you up."

"No need. You go and get Sally some ice cream. I bet she sleeps well tonight."

"I'm sure she'll sleep better than I will. See you Monday?"

His attempt at humor made her heart ache. "Of course. Well, I'll let you go." She got out of the car and pulled in a deep cleansing breath that she hoped would hold her in good stead. At least until she got into the house. Closed the door. And cried her eyes out.

CHAPTER TWELVE

A KNOCK ON his office door sounded Tuesday morning. He smiled. That was probably Mysti. He'd tried calling her several times, but the call kept going to voice mail. And he hadn't seen her at work at all yesterday, but then again, he'd been slammed with patients.

She'd seemed to be acting so oddly when he'd taken her home, but he'd finally chalked that up to his own paranoia. Because she hadn't acted strange while they were out on the water earlier. She'd been playful, and they'd even sneaked in little touches here and there.

"Come in."

The door opened. It wasn't Mysti, though. It was the hospital administrator. He blinked.

"Hi, Tom. What can I do for you?"

"I'm not sure." His words rolled out slowly. "Have you heard anything about Dr. North wanting to move out of the area? HR just contacted me saying they'd gotten a call from Doctors Without Borders asking for job and character references. And she's taken today and tomorrow as personal days."

It took him a minute to process what he was hearing. Then he pushed his chair back in a daze, an ugly feeling of déjà vu pressing at his midsection.

"She what?"

Tom shrugged. "She hasn't formally given notice yet, but I think I see the writing on the wall. She still has quite a bit of time on her contract left. Any idea what's going on?"

"No. Sorry."

Except he did. She was heading out of town, just like that. Just like she'd done the last time. She hadn't given him any notice that time, either, just said she was leaving. And that was that. He hadn't seen her again after that night in the car.

So why had she acted the way she had on the boat? All soft and smiley, warm and affectionate. She'd won his daughter's heart over already. Sally had asked about her all weekend long.

Damn her! It was one thing to play with his heart. It was another thing altogether to toy with his daughter's affections like that.

Tom shrugged. "Okay, well, if you hear

of anything, let me know, will you? We'd like to fix whatever is wrong if possible. I'd hate to lose her. She's excellent with her patients and a damn good surgeon, from what I'm told."

"Yes. She's both of those things."

But what she wasn't...was honest.

Wait a minute. She played it straight when you asked her if she was staying. She told you she wasn't sure.

But he'd sure as hell thought she'd at least work out her contract.

After what she'd been through, though, could he blame her? Maybe it was too hard to face the people she'd known before her military days. Maybe after telling him what she'd been through, she'd decided she couldn't play twenty questions with every friend and old acquaintance who asked about her scars. To relive that pain over and over and over. Even he had made a big deal about them, going as far as touching the ones on her shoulder as they'd headed to the lake.

Maybe going where everyone was a stranger was preferable.

"I'll let you know if she says anything to me."

Otherwise, he was keeping his mouth

shut. He wasn't going to spread gossip about Mysti or anyone.

And if she'd wanted him to know she was leaving, surely she would have told him. So was she just planning to ghost him?

Why not? A terrible voice in his head jeered. *It's exactly what she did last time.*

Go after her. Ask her.

He didn't think so. He'd tried to call her already, and she hadn't responded. Now he knew why. He wasn't going to track her down and beg to know what was going on. If she'd wanted him to know, she would have returned his calls. Maybe she'd just realized that she couldn't handle a relationship. Not now. Not with him.

If that were the case, he needed to respect that decision.

So what was he going to tell Sally?

The truth. That Mysti had decided to change jobs and had to move. Far away.

Where he would probably never see her again.

His throat squeezed tight.

His daughter would be sad for a little while, but she'd get over it, especially with school and all the other activities she had. And him?

He didn't rebound as easily these days.

Jesse barely noticed Tom letting himself out of his office. Instead he squared up his jaw and picked up his next patient's file. It was the only thing he could do. No matter how he felt, his personal life had no business intruding during office hours. His patients deserved all his skill and attention.

And that's exactly what they were going to get.

Jesse lasted a whole three days. And last night, he'd stayed awake unable to sleep, playing back what had happened on that trip last weekend over and over in his mind. It made no sense. But he was damned if he was going to spend night after night torturing himself with whatever he'd done wrong this time.

He'd said he wouldn't beg her to stay, and he wouldn't. But what he could do was go see her face-to-face and ask her why she'd decided to contact Doctors Without Borders without telling him. Why she still hadn't been back to work since their day out.

Was he going to go to her house and admit he'd listened to what boiled down to as gossip?

Well, it wasn't exactly gossip if Tom had

said the nonprofit had already contacted the hospital about her.

But maybe this time, Jesse could at least gain some closure. Closure that he hadn't gotten last time because of his own crazy feelings about kissing her. His fear of repeating his dad's mistakes had held him back from pursuing Mysti that time. He hadn't sought her or Kandid out to try to explain things.

But he hadn't cheated on his wife, damn it. He hadn't been happy with her, but he suspected she hadn't been happy, either. Even after discovering she'd cheated on him, he'd stayed in the marriage because of her illness. Because of their daughter. And he wasn't sorry he had. Because there, at least, he'd had closure. He'd been able to say goodbye.

What he was sorry for, though, was not tracking down Mysti and talking through with her what had happened. He'd cared about her back then. Had probably even loved her, although he hadn't realized it.

Was he going to make that same mistake this time? Let her walk away without a word? Or was he going to do one of the hardest things he'd ever done in his life and go to her and admit that he loved her?

If she didn't feel the same way, that would

be that. But he'd at least have the peace of knowing he'd tried.

Larry's example of living life to the fullest because "none of us knows how long we'll travel this earth" had stuck in his head ever since they'd sat out on that lake together in the tournament. Larry had given them a thumbs-up sign that day. He'd been happy. Had done what he loved doing. Until the very end.

Jesse had the chance now to do exactly that. And this time, he wasn't going to let the opportunity pass him by while he sat in his office and did nothing.

He was done with his patients today, so he closed the files he'd been working on and slid them into the top drawer of his desk. Then he closed out his computer and called his mom, asking her if she could pick up Sally from school. If she could keep her for the night.

"Of course, you know I love having my grandbaby with me. Is everything okay?"

"Yes. I just need to spend some time with a friend."

He hung up and left the hospital, getting in his car and driving to a place he hoped might hold the answers he was looking for.

It didn't take him long to get to her house. Her car was parked out front. The crops in the fields surrounding the house had turned it into a little green oasis. There were marigolds planted in the small bed out front, and the window boxes boasted their own greenery. This didn't look like a house that was about to be abandoned.

He rang the bell and waited. No phone calls this time. If she was leaving, she was going to have to tell him to his face.

The door swung open, and she stood there for a second before her head tilted and she frowned. "Jess?"

"Can we talk?"

She licked her lips, but nodded and stepped aside. "I— It's good that you're here, because I actually need to tell you something."

Here it came. She was going to tell him she was leaving—going overseas again, this time with Doctors Without Borders.

Forever.

Because if he lost her this time, he knew in his heart of hearts he would never have another chance with her. So he was going down the hard road. Not the easy road. Not this time.

He moved through the doorway, and the

first thing he saw were boxes. Moving boxes. None of them were taped shut, but most of them had stuff in them. "So it's true. You're leaving. Tom said HR had gotten a request for your employment information."

"This has been a difficult decision." Her eyes shut for a second before opening. She looked agonized. "Let's sit down."

"No. I'd rather have this out right here. I'm done wasting time. So just tell me clear and plain. Yes or no. Are you leaving?"

"I was going to."

"Was? Does that mean you've changed your mind?"

She sighed heavily. "That depends."

That was not the answer he'd expected. "On what, exactly?"

"On your answer to a question."

He had no idea what she was talking about. But it sounded like he had indeed done something wrong on that outing. He just had no damn idea what. "Okay. What's your question?"

She bit her lip. "I really do need to sit down for this."

Leading the way over to a small love seat, she motioned for him to sit. He did. But instead of going over to the chair across from it, she actually sat down beside him, turning toward him. "Are you still in love with Kandid?"

"What?" he asked incredulously. He leaned back against the back cushion trying to read her face. "What does Kandid have to do with whether or not you leave?"

"Everything." Her chin wobbled for a second before going still. "Kandid has everything to do with it. I saw it all, you know, in your garage."

His garage?

His head spun for a few seconds, and suddenly he realized exactly what this was about. Why she'd changed so suddenly at the end of their day together.

Hell, looking at it through her eyes...

"This is all because of Kandid's things still being out there."

She nodded. "After that night at your house, I thought that...well, I thought you might be able to move forward."

Mysti rolled her shoulder, and he wanted to stop her. To touch her and ease the way. Because he knew exactly what that nervous gesture meant. She was struggling with something and wasn't sure of the outcome. He wanted to grab her and tell her everything was going to be okay. But right now, he couldn't promise her that, because he still wasn't sure it would be.

"I care deeply about you, Mysti. That garage..." How could he explain it so that she would understand?

"You care about me. But you don't love me." Before he could even respond to that, she went on. "You chose Kandid over me that night in your car, and I'm honestly not sure I can—or even if I want to—compete with that. I need it to be *me* that you see when you take me to bed. *Me* that you see when I'm holding Sally. Kandid's gone, and I'm so sorry you lost her. But I can't be her replacement. I *won't* be her replacement."

He reached for her hand and held it tightly. "God, Mysti, that has never even crossed my mind, and I'm sorry if I ever made you feel that way. That night in the car..." He tried to sort through his chaotic memories of that time. "I was dating Kandid, but that kiss of ours just blew me away. And the thought that came immediately on its heels stunned me—I wondered if that was how my father felt when he kissed women who weren't his wife. It just about killed me."

"I told you the truth back then. You're nothing like him."

"Maybe, but at the time, that fear consumed me until I couldn't think straight. It kept me from coming after you. Kept me from contacting you after you left town."

He went on. "I made such a mess out of things back then. I made a mess with Kandid, too. I was not a good husband to her. I didn't cheat. But I held back from her emotionally. I think I finally know why." He took her face in his hands. "It was because of you. And I think that is why I held on to all of Kandid's things—guilt."

If Mysti could confess the secret about her friend who'd died, he could confess his own secret. "I kept them all because I felt guilty. A couple of years into my marriage, I realized I didn't love Kandid the way I should. But I was determined to prove to myself that—unlike my father—I fulfilled my commitments no matter what the cost. And I did. But in doing so I made us both miserable. And then Sally came along and later, Kandid got sick… Well, I told myself I was keeping that stuff so that someday our daughter could look through it and choose what she wanted. But that wasn't it. I hadn't made Kandid happy in our marriage, and I was ashamed. That is the awful truth of it."

Mysti stared at him as the silence grew from a few seconds to a full minute.

"Oh, Jesse. I'm so sorry. I just assumed you couldn't bear to let her go. But *my* sad truth is something I realized just this morning. I can't bear to let *you* go."

His eyes widened as he gazed at her. Had she really just said that? "You can't bear to let me go?"

"No. And I decided something else, just now. I'm not leaving Forgotten Point again, even if you don't feel the same way about me."

A strange thumping began in his chest. "And what is it you feel?"

She leaned her cheek into his palm. "I feel love. I love you, Jess."

He sat there frozen for a second before snatching her to him, squeezing her against his chest as he tried to contain the emotions that were tearing through him. "You've just said the words I thought I'd never hear."

"So…you…you…"

"Yes. I love you. I think I loved you in the car all of those years ago. I was just too immature to realize it. And too cowardly to stop and think things through."

Her lips pressed against his throat. "Hmm… that kiss was a funny thing, because I definitely had a crush on you back then. What

I feel now is no crush, though. It's the real thing."

Hope poured over him in a cleansing stream that washed away old regrets. That made everything seem brand-new.

"I promise you, mine is the real thing, too. So what are we going to do about it?"

She pulled back and looked into his face. "Oh, no! What time is it? Do we need to go get Sally from school?"

We? Had she just said *we*? He couldn't believe how much he loved the sound of that.

"My mom is picking her up, actually. Sally's going to spend the night with her. Because I wasn't sure how long this was going to take."

"As promising as that last part sounds, I'm a little disappointed we can't tell her that she was right."

He cocked his head. "Right about what?"

"That her dad finally has a girlfriend." She said it in a singsong voice that had laughter flowing through every note.

Oh, how he loved this woman.

"I think she's going to be very happy to hear that." He kissed her mouth. "And so am I. So I have a girlfriend, do I? I was kind of hoping for a little more than that."

"You were? What kind of things were you hoping for?"

He brushed the hair back from her face. "I think it might take me a while to list them all. A long while, in fact. Interested in some company tonight?"

"Definitely." She smiled and rubbed her fingers across his jaw. "Stubble. I love it. Love feeling this at the end of your work-day."

"I'm glad, because I think you're stuck with it. And with me." He leaned down to kiss her again. "What do you suggest we do with ourselves tonight?"

She made a humming sound in her throat. "I think I know the perfect thing. The thing that will set our union in stone."

He liked the sound of that. So did his body. It began to think through all kinds of scenarios. "I'm listening."

"The one big thing I need you to do for me…" She trailed her fingertip down his chest and swirled a big circle around one of his nipples. "That would make my whole world come alive…"

"Yes?" The word came out in hoarse expectation.

"Is help me unpack all of these boxes."

She laughed at the expression he must have made. "But only after we go and figure out who'll be in the driver's seat tonight."

EPILOGUE

"ARE YOU SURE we should be out here?"

Mysti smiled and linked her fingers through his. "I told you. I'm fine." She leaned her head against his shoulder. "But I have to tell you, you're driving like an old grandpa right now."

"Ow." He pressed his hand to his chest as if her words had found their mark.

Glancing back at where Sally was lounging on a cushion in her life vest, the little girl chortled. "Mimi called you a grandpa."

Her throat swelled with so much love, she couldn't speak for several seconds. They'd decided on what Sally would call her at a family meeting the day before they got married. And every time the little girl called her Mimi, she wanted to grab her and hug her until she squealed.

"That's right, I did. And if he keeps going this slowly it'll take us all day to get to our fishing spot."

The first annual Larry Rogers Memorial Fish-Off was already a roaring success. Larry's son had cut the ribbon on the bronze statue of a man in his boat, fishing line cast in the water. A tribute to the man who'd loved to be out on this lake.

Jesse growled. "I'm not taking any chances with either of my girls. Nor the new little one you have growing inside you."

"The obstetrician gave us a green light to be out here."

His brows went up. "'As long as you don't do anything crazy.' Don't forget that part."

"Not much chance of that, is there?" She popped him with her hip. "Move over. I'm driving."

"Um… No. You got to drive last night."

The pointed reference to their passionate lovemaking the night before made her laugh. "Only because you were driving like a grandpa then, too."

"Oh, ho. We'll have to see about that, Mysti." But he stepped out of the way and motioned toward the wheel. "I'm warning you, though. You have precious cargo on board."

Suddenly she couldn't see through a rush of tears. Yes, she did. Sally and Jesse were definitely precious cargo. As was the baby that was due this winter. They almost didn't make it to this point. Had almost let go of everything that mattered.

But they hadn't. They'd stayed and fought for each other, fought for the chance to bond into a new family. One built on all the right things: love. Commitment. Sacrifice.

Mysti had stayed on at the hospital when the doctor on maternity leave decided against returning. And she wasn't sure yet what she was going to do when her own baby came. Jesse had suggested they form a new practice, saying it was the perfect partnership.

She couldn't agree more.

And although Jesse said he regretted not going after her all those years ago, maybe he'd been right not to. They'd both grown into two mature adults who were ready to love each other in a way they might not have been able to back then.

So she held out her hand to him, maintaining the boat at the speed he'd originally set. When Jesse gripped her fingers and moved closer, kissing her left shoulder, where those scars lay hidden beneath her shirt, she sighed.

"Precious cargo. I love that. We all are, though, aren't we?" As she looked at her family, her next words were a vow that she hoped Larry could somehow hear. "For as long as we travel this earth."

* * * * *

If you enjoyed this story, check out these other great reads from Tina Beckett

The Trouble with the Tempting Doc
How to Win the Surgeon's Heart
Consequences of Their New York Night
It Started with a Winter Kiss

All available now!